I0546167

ROKUL

CONQUERED WORLD: BOOK EIGHT

ELIN WYN

CLOCK
WALK
PUBLISHING

TELLA

I've never believed in expectations.

The way I see it, expectations only guarantee the promise of disappointment.

I approached Rigkon with absolutely zero expectations, yet somehow still managed to be disappointed.

Rigkon was a new town. A bunch of them were springing up all over Ankou as more displaced refugees needed homes. The Xathi had done more damage than I initially realized. Rigkon was near where Fraga used to be.

There were plans in the works to rebuild Fraga, but it wasn't a priority at the moment. The capital city, Nyheim, was still in the process of rebuilding. Progress was moving quickly, but it was a big city.

Small, currently useless cities, like Fraga, would have to wait.

Rigkon had an identity crisis. It wanted to be an outpost for construction crews when the time came to start rebuilding Fraga. It also wanted to be part of Fraga when the time came.

There was a handful of squat bungalows where the twenty or so permanent residents lived, a sad market with three half-empty stalls, and a long squat building that looked suspiciously like a bar.

I didn't get my hopes up. I couldn't live with the disappointment if it turned out to be something else.

If I hadn't decided to cram this gig in before starting my lab job, I'd never have known this place was here.

Before the Xathi invasion, this area was nothing but thick forest occasionally punctuated by a picturesque clearing that could've been lovely for picnics if it weren't for the aggressive flora. The Xathi had ravaged the landscape as they tore from human settlement to human settlement.

Rigkon's developers barely had to clear out any trees to make the faint dirt trail that served as the only road, not that anyone here had need of a road. I guessed it was an attempt to make the little outpost look more official.

For all of its faults, Rigkon had one thing going for it.

It was a botanist's heaven.

That's what had brought me here in the first place. I saw an ad for a small job and took it on a whim. I needed the extra cash.

I still didn't have quite enough for my own place, even though I was due to start a stable job soon. It would be my first one since before the Xathi invasion. Since I'd be in the area, I'd promised an old contact a consult on a different project once I got to town.

But that wasn't until...

Wait, shit.

I checked the date reader strapped around my wrist. It was frozen, like it had been for two days. Rigkon didn't have any transmission signal.

It wasn't part of the shuttle system, either. I wish I'd known that before taking the job. I'd been walking along old roads and hitching rides for a day and a half now.

I was supposed to start my new job at the lab today.

Before I came out here, I sent a message to the lab where I'd recently been hired. I mentioned that I'd be coming out to Rigkon on a one-time gig, but should be back in time to start on the agreed date. Now I had no chance of getting a message through out here. And I hadn't thought to message my contact about the other project.

I couldn't resist this gig. It was one of the few opportunities offering fieldwork. I lived for fieldwork.

I wasn't meant to be cooped up in a lab squinting into vials, monitors, and datasheets. It was a pity fieldwork didn't pay as well as lab jobs.

I would at least be gathering hazard pay.

I pulled out my datapad and checked the info I'd been sent when I accepted the job in Rigkon. It didn't say much other than I was supposed to meet a man called Gille in a place called Crooked Swiggen.

I squinted against the sunlight, looking for anything that bore such an odd name. Sure enough, that squat little building had a faded C above the doorway. Since I didn't see anything else that could be the Crooked Swiggen, I made my way over.

The door didn't fill the doorway. There was about a foot of space between the top of the doorway and the top of the door. There was a similar gap at the base of the door, as well. There wasn't a doorknob or a handle. I bumped the door with my knee, letting it swing into the darkened interior of the Crooked Swiggen.

I'd never seen a sorrier-looking bar.

A slab of wood lined with mismatched barstools took up the wall to my left. Whoever owned this place had built shelves big enough to hold an impressive amount of spirits, however, there were less than ten bottles on display. Over half of them were empty.

A few mismatched chairs and tables dotted the dirty floor. Only one table was occupied. Two men with skin as dark and wrinkled as tree bark hunched over matching mugs of something or other. They didn't look up when I entered, leaving me to assume that the lone man sitting at the bar was Gille.

His pants were so dusty, I couldn't tell what color they had once been. His work boots were splattered with thick mud. He'd obviously been out in the forest recently. Gille's skin was dark from many hours spent under the sun. His chin was covered with dark stubble speckled with flecks of silver.

Gille had a disappointing face. Nothing remarkable whatsoever. If I saw him in a crowd, I wouldn't be able to pick him out.

"Are you lost?" he asked blandly when I approached.

"Unfortunately, I'm not." I placed my bag on the bar and hopped up onto one of the stools. It felt like it was going to fall apart under my weight. "You Gille?"

"Yeah." He looked confused, yet still managed to give me a once over.

I rolled my eyes. I wanted to order a drink, but Gille likely wanted me to start working right away. I didn't want to have anything in my system when I went out in the forest.

"I'm Tella Briar, your botanist," I clarified.

Gille had the audacity to scoff.

I glared at him. "What?"

"I wasn't expecting a woman, that's all. Not a lot of female botanists work outside of labs these days." At least he was honest.

"Yeah, I'm a real treasure," I quipped. "Tell me more about the job. Your ad was pretty sparse."

"I didn't want to scare off prospective takers," Gilles replied. He took a long swig of whatever foul-smelling drink he had.

"That's not a good sign." I couldn't help but feel excited. This was exactly what I was looking for. "Tell me the details."

"We've had some unusual encounters with kodanos," Gilles explained. "They've been making life hard for us. One destroyed a food shipment last week. We had to live off potatoes and beet stew until the next one came. There's a particular kodanos out there that's terrorizing unarmed shipments."

"That doesn't seem very unusual," I frowned.

"It's hard to explain. They seem angry or something, but this one kodanos has just gone crazy. This guy is terrorizing anything and everything that moves." Gille muttered into the bar. "Anyway, it doesn't matter. I'm not giving you the job. It's too dangerous for a little thing like you to go up against it."

Without thinking about it, I reached for the hilt of my hunting knife and gripped it hard. I wasn't going to stab him or anything, but I wouldn't mind him knowing I could.

"Have you had many replies for your ad?" I asked.

Gille didn't answer, which was answer enough for me.

"Okay," I shrugged. "Hope you like potato and beet stew."

"Wait," Gille said quickly. "If you really think you can handle that kodanos, I'll hire you. If you get hurt, it's not my problem."

"Pay me half now and half when I get back." I took my datapad out of my bag and dropped it in front of him. He looked at me to see if I was joking. I lifted one brow.

"Fine." He transferred half of the payment into my account and slid the datapad back to me.

"Thanks." I smiled brightly and tucked the datapad away. "Any place where I can get some supplies?"

"Market's in the lot next to this place. There's a store on the other side of the market." Gille spoke without looking at me. I knew I'd been dismissed. I left the bar feeling excited. I didn't know Rigkon had a shop.

This would be easy money. Kodanos were a walk in the park for me. I'd handled dozens, maybe even hundreds.

The supply store was just as grimy and dark as the Crooked Swiggen. Bunches of dried plants hung from the ceiling. Chipped and broken knickknacks lined the crooked shelves. I didn't see a shopkeeper.

I moved farther into the store, looking for anything that might be useful.

A dented canteen caught my eye. I'd lost mine moving around after the invasion, so I snagged it. I could probably fill it at the Crooked Swiggen. After another loop around the shop, I didn't find anything besides the canteen. Still, there was no shopkeeper to be seen. I stepped up to the register, thinking there might be a bell or something. There wasn't.

"Hello?" I called out, though I knew I wouldn't get an answer. There wasn't a backroom in this shop. After waiting a few more minutes, I left the shop with the canteen in hand.

The three stalls at the market were occupied. I walked up to the first one, manned by a large woman with a wide, friendly face.

"Excuse me, do you know who runs the shop?" I asked. "I want to buy this."

"Oh, I run it, dear!" she said brightly. "I saw you go in. I figured you'd come looking for me. I have a good sense about people."

"Right." I wasn't sure what to say. "How much?"

The woman's smile never faded as she rung me up. I wondered if she consciously forced herself to keep her smile on or if she genuinely was that happy.

"Thanks." I nodded and walked away.

As I passed the last stall, something caught my eye. Amidst the sparse piece of useless junk was a silver dart. The base of the dart was filled with deep red liquid.

"What's this?" I asked.

"Toxins from the glands of Narrisiri," the stall keeper said. My eyes lit up.

"I'll take it!" I didn't care how much it cost.

Narrisiri toxin was hard to come by. I tucked the dart into a safe place in my utility bag. After stopping back into the Crooked Swiggen for some water, I marched into the thick forest, eager to be in my element once again.

ROKUL

"General Rouhr just called us in for a meeting."

I looked up. It was my brother, Takar. He had a habit of walking into my room without knocking.

If it was anyone else, it would've angered me, but Takar and I had shared a room for most of our lives. In fact, this was the first time we'd had separate rooms.

We lived in a run-down building on the outskirts of Nyheim. It was one of the few buildings in the capital city that still had its original walls. The Xathi just barely missed this one, which wasn't actually a good thing. The landlady, a tiny human woman named Hellin, was nearly one hundred years of age would be buried up to her frail neck in repair bills making it safe again.

In addition to paying our rent, Takar and I fixed whatever we could for her so she wouldn't have to hire someone. It seemed like the least we could do. Most of the humans on Ankou weren't afraid of us anymore, but that didn't mean they were opening their homes for us to permanently reside.

When Hellin first saw us, two tall Skotan brothers loaded with weapons, she didn't even flinch. That's how we knew this would work out.

By now, Hellin doted on us as if we were kin.

I didn't mind humans, I thought they were fragile, and maybe a little stupid, but not Hellin. I'd kill for Hellin if she said the word.

"What about?" I asked.

"What do you think?" Takar gave me the look he's been giving me since we were children and he realized he was the smart one.

"Giant killer plant?" Takar nodded.

Yes.

I bet General Rouhr was finally ready to authorize an attack on the gigantic sentient plant we'd apparently awakened during our final battle with the Xathi.

I didn't fully understand what it was, none of us did. My strike team leader, Karzin, was one of the first people to see it, though he didn't get a good look. All we knew was that it was incalculably large, secreted a memory-altering gas, and was capable of attacking human settlements without warning from under the ground.

When it first began its attacks, there were sometimes as many as three a day. There were human casualties, but not nearly as many as there had been when the Xathi invaded. Less than thirty humans had lost their lives in these attacks.

Now, the attacks seemed to have slowed.

No one knew why.

And that wasn't comforting at all.

"When's the meeting?" I asked.

"Right now." Takar was ready to go. He made a show of looking impatient while I scrambled to get my gear together.

He might be smarter, he might be more organized and logical, but I was the better warrior. There was no contest.

Takar even admitted it once, though he said it was only because I acted before I considered consequences.

I wouldn't say he was wrong.

Our lodging was a ten-minute walk from General Rouhr's fancy new office. Our operation had two floors to itself, as well as a lab. I wasn't sure what was on the other floors. I didn't care, honestly.

We were the last ones to arrive. General Rouhr looked annoyed.

"Now that the rest of my team is here," Karzin gave Takar and me a pointed look, "are we ready to begin?"

"Dr. Dewitt, has your associate arrived?" General

Rouhr asked the petite blonde doctor who even I'd be hesitant to go against in a fight.

Leena's sharp mouth grew tight.

"No," she said, clearly irked. "Apparently, Dr. Briar left a message nearly two days ago telling the laboratory about doing a quick job in Rigkon, and she must've gotten sidetracked."

"What is she talking about?" I whispered to Karzin.

"Weren't you listening at the last meeting?" Karzin lifted his brows.

"I must've forgotten," I grinned. Karzin rolled his eyes.

"Leena has a colleague who's supposedly some kind of botanical expert. The general thinks the botanist can help us understand what we're up against," Karzin explained.

"Why are we bringing in some botanist?" I asked.

"Do you have an objection, Rokul?" General Rouhr said.

"Uh." I stood up straight. "No, sir. I was simply curious. If we're looking for information about this plant-thing, wouldn't Jeneva be the appropriate candidate for such a job?"

"Jeneva's a naturalist," Leena cut in. "She can tell us everything under the sun about known plant species, but she can't tell us much about new ones. And brilliant as she is, she doesn't have much official laboratory training that could also assist us with this puzzle."

"Exactly," General Rouhr nodded, but I could tell there was more to it. There was a hint of worry in his eyes.

"Is that all, sir?" I asked, though it wasn't my place. Then again, I was never one for staying in my place.

"Since you're all bound to find out anyway, I might as well tell you now." General Rouhr nodded solemnly. "Jeneva is experiencing some complications with her pregnancy."

Concerned murmurs spread throughout the room and I felt guilty for bringing it up. All of us were fond of Jeneva. She was plucky. I liked that in a friend. I suddenly felt bad for not talking to her as much as I should've.

"Will she be okay?" Karzin asked.

"Yes," General Rouhr nodded. "She just needs to be on bedrest most of the day. She is, after all, the first human to carry a Skotan child. There's bound to be some complications."

That was most likely a massive understatement. Skotan babies develop their scales in the womb and the period of formation is quite uncomfortable for Skotan females. It must be even more uncomfortable for human females.

With a shudder, I put it out of my mind.

She was a tough woman. She would be fine.

I hoped.

"Did you say that botanist isn't here?" I asked Leena, who nodded curtly. "Shouldn't we explore alternate methods of dealing with that thing out in the desert?"

"Do you want to run this meeting, Rokul?" General Rouhr asked. "You certainly seem to have a lot of ideas."

"We're restless, General!" I threw my hands up. "We've known about this thing for over a week. It's killing people and destroying buildings, yet somehow, it's still alive. Why aren't we out there tearing it to shreds and protecting our planet?"

"You're out of line," General Rouhr warned me.

"I apologize, General. I simply don't see what a gardener with access to a fancy lab can do to help us solve this problem, especially when we have an arsenal at our disposal," I countered.

"Rokul," Takar muttered in warning.

"Don't scold me for wanting answers," I snapped. "Karzin, Annie is a sweet female and she's very smart. I'm impressed with the information she was able to uncover, but I don't see what more information we need. We know the thing is dangerous, we know it's toxic. Why not take it out with a well-executed aerial attack?"

"How do we kill it?" General Rouhr asked. "You

seem to have thought everything through. Tell me how to kill it."

"A couple of grenades will kill just about anything," I shrugged.

"And if that doesn't work? We'll have lost some grenades and angered that thing even more," General Rouhr replied. "What are the consequences of killing such a massive creature that may be deeply entangled with the planet?"

"We won't have to deal with that thing attacking cities and wiping people's memories," I said.

"What will happen to the integrity of the land mass, removing something so large?" General Rouhr asked. "How will it affect the ecosystem? Man-made resources are in short supply thanks to the Xathi destroying a large part of Duvest's manufacturing district. The humans are relying on natural resources now more than ever. Will killing this creature affect that?"

"Why would it?" I scoffed.

"I don't know, but do you know for a fact that it won't?" General Rouhr demanded.

"I suppose not," I replied reluctantly.

"Now you know why we need more information. Killing this creature might do more harm than good. In such a turbulent time, we can't afford to make any mistakes," General Rouhr said.

"I, and the rest of the humans, appreciate the

sentiment, General," Leena smiled. "However, my friend isn't here and we still have to come up with something."

"Do you know any other botanists?" General Rouhr asked.

"No, but I can ask around. Maybe some of my old colleagues from the university know someone else," Leena suggested.

"Great. Get working on that. Where did you say your friend went?"

"Rigkon. I've never heard of it," Leena shrugged.

"It's an outpost of sorts," Vidia, General Rouhr's human mate, spoke up. Since the Xathi were defeated, Vidia has been at the forefront of rebuilding human settlements.

"Of sorts?" General Rouhr repeated.

"It was meant to be the first step in rebuilding Fraga, but funds had to be redirected at the last minute." I didn't miss the hint of sadness in her voice. Vidia used to be the mayor of Fraga. I wasn't entirely sure what that meant, exactly. Skotan governments didn't have anything like it. But I knew that it was a person of importance and I knew she took the destruction of Fraga hard.

"Ah," General Rouhr said softly. "Well, in that case, since we know where it is, I'm going to send someone to retrieve this botanist."

Personally, I didn't think it was worth the trouble. Unfortunately for me, my thoughts must've been written all over my face.

"Rokul." The general's voice was too perky and his smile was too big. That never, ever boded well for anyone. "I think this is exactly the sort of job you're suited for."

"An errand job?" I tried not to scoff. I was already in enough trouble.

"Yes," General Rouhr replied. "It'll give you some time to get to know our new colleague. Perhaps the botanist can help you understand why we can't just blow up the creature out in the desert, since I'm not getting through to you."

"Yes, sir," I muttered.

Beside me, my brother and the rest of my strike team tried to hold back their laughter, and failed.

TELLA

The forest looked like it'd been strangled. The leaves weren't as vibrant as they used to be. The canopy used to be so thick that it was impossible to see the sky. When I looked up now, the canopy was more sky than plant life.

Since the canopy was so fragmented, much more heat was able to pierce down to the forest floor. The temperature of the whole forest was elevated. Quite a few native plants weren't meant to cope with such high temperatures. I bent down to examine the crinkled, dry remains of what was once a Pallidia flower. Ordinarily, that flower was the size of my face. Now, the dried-up petals fit into the palm of my hand.

I stood up and let the petals fall back down to the forest floor.

My footfalls were too loud now that this section had dried out so much, and I tried to walk as quietly as possible to avoid drawing attention to myself.

Before the Xathi attack, this area of forest had been particularly hazardous.

When humans first settled on Ankou, the forest seemed the most promising location to settle due to rainfall and abundant resources. It didn't take our forefathers long to figure out that the lush forest was filled to the brim with creatures pulled from a nightmare.

Our forest had two giant species of sentient trees, flowers as large as a grown man with a taste for blood, and vines that silently stalked people as they ventured into the depths of the forest.

It's amazing that any of the first settlers survived long enough to reproduce.

As I went over the catalog of flora and fauna native to this part of the forest, I realized something unsettling.

The forest was silent.

Before the Xathi attack, it sounded like every creature in the forest was right on top of you at all times. There was always something rustling, hissing, or growling. The sentient trees sounded like thunderstorms when they moved.

Forests like this weren't supposed to be quiet. I

wondered if the Xathi slaughtered the wildlife as well as the humans, or if the wildlife migrated before the Xathi came through.

Something glinting in the light caught my eye. My heart clenched in my chest. I stumbled backward.

Half buried in dead leaves was a fragment of a Xathi's leg.

I liked to think that nothing in this forest could scare me, but the sight of that leg shook me to my core. I gave the leg a wide berth and changed direction. I didn't want to turn my back on that thing. The Xathi tried to kill my race, they tried to kill this forest, and they'd very nearly succeeded in destroying us all.

I walked for nearly a full hour before I heard signs of life. The unmistakable crack of wood snapping against wood echoed through the forest. I grinned and quickened my pace.

I enjoyed fieldwork. I liked the element of danger. I liked harvesting my own samples for analysis in a lab. I liked controlling every step of the process. However, I'd never been so excited to hear a sentient tree that I rushed toward it.

I expected to find kodanos and I was not disappointed. However, I was alarmed. The kodanos tore at another tree, a non-sentient tree, with speed and ferocity I'd never seen before.

Kodanos were the larger of the two species of

sentient tree. Their limbs were massive and heavy. They usually moved much more slowly.

I crouched low and held very still.

Kodanos didn't have eyes. They relied on the tiny but incredibly sensitive fibers that covered their body to sense even the tiniest movement. If the kodanos was behaving normally, it would've sensed me long before I spotted it.

But perhaps, since it was moving so erratically, it couldn't feel me? Something wasn't right.

Kodanos might've been the bigger of the two species, but it was the less aggressive.

Normally.

As I watched it tear into the regular tree until only a stump remained, I wondered what it was doing. And why. It took a lot of effort for a kodanos to move its body. It wouldn't do something like that without reason.

Something gave out beneath my feet. I must've been standing on a dried-out branch or root. The snap it made was the loudest noise in the forest beside the kodanos. It twisted its gnarled body in my direction. Its delicate filaments flared red, though it was hardly visible in the harsh light of day.

I held my breath, but that didn't matter. It knew I was here. I kept as still as possible. Hopefully, it would decide I wasn't worth the energy.

Instead, it charged at me faster than I'd ever seen an ordinary kodanos move.

I didn't think twice.

I ran for my life.

I pelted through the forest, barely dodging the trees. Branches caught in my hair and slashed at my face. As the kodanos continued to hunt me, I noticed something else unusual about its behavior. Within the central chamber of a kodanos's body was usually a hive of live talusians, small winged reptiles with needle-like teeth and toxic saliva.

If a kodanos decided that a target was worth perusing, it released a swarm of talusians. The two lifeforms worked in an elegant, lethal symbiosis.

Yet as I ran, I didn't hear the telltale hiss of wings.

I'd begun to think that I'd discovered a new species of kodanos when I spied a gnarled tree, perfect for climbing. I leaped onto the trunk and scrambled up into the branches just as the kodanos collided with the tree.

Kodanos couldn't climb, but this one refused to give up. It started to tear and slash at this tree just like it had the other one. The tree shivered and thrashed from the assault. It wouldn't be long before this tree came down, too.

My options were limited, but I had to think fast.

I grabbed the hilt of my hunting knife and pulled it

loose. If I timed this correctly, I might live long enough to see the inside of the lab.

Never thought that would sound like a good plan.

I took a deep breath and leaped down from the tree, pushing off hard enough that I would sail clear over the kodanos.

I twisted in the air and, as I fell, I drove my knife into the wooden knot at the top of the kodanos's back. The blade drove in down to the hilt. I gripped the hilt with both hands and used my body weight to pull the knife down its spine.

It worked for about a foot before the knife slipped free and I slammed onto the forest floor.

The kodanos arched its back and let out a shrill cry. It waved its thick arms, trying to claw at the fresh wound on its back. Thick black sap burst from the new gash like a geyser. While it thrashed in pain, I lashed out with my knife again.

This time, I buried it deep within its leg joint. One sharp twist of my hand, and black sap began to spurt out from the joint. I pulled the knife back and jabbed again. My blade was almost completely through its leg.

Using the gash I'd already created, I threw my weight against the hilt. Wood gave out beneath my blade. The bottom half of the kodanos's leg snapped. Its bulky body lost balance. I scrambled away, dead leaves clinging to my sap-covered hands as I went.

The impact of the kodanos hitting the earth reverberated through my body. Though it was down, it still fought. I knew it would never stand up again, not with one of its legs hanging on by a twig. It had fallen on its front. Its vulnerable back was exposed.

I got to my feet and took off running. With one bound, I landed on the kodanos's back. It flailed beneath me, but its arms couldn't reach me.

"I'm sorry," I murmured before driving my knife through its head. It gave a final shudder, then fell motionless.

There were two aspects to botany in this world. There was the part in the lab looking through microscopes and running experiments. This was the other part. It wasn't a surprise that many botanists didn't enjoy fieldwork.

I still loved it.

My hands were trembling, but not with fear, with adrenaline. I lived for this rush.

I didn't like killing the kodanos, however, that was the job I'd agreed to do. I didn't imagine it would be like this, though. What was wrong with this one? I'd thought Gille was exaggerating, maybe just a city idiot who didn't know any better.

But there was something terribly wrong here.

I decided to open it up and take a look for myself. The inside of a plant, especially a sentient one, always said more about it than the outside. I cracked open the hard bark shell of its back and chipped away at it until I could see inside.

I'd never seen anything like it before. The insides of the kodanos were twisted up with the vines of some other plant. Even the talusians' hive was crushed beneath the vines. A few dried-up dead talusians had spilled out of the hive and were just sitting there inside the gullet of the kodanos.

Did those vines come from some kind of invasive species?

Perhaps the kodanos accidentally ingested a seed and the vines sprouted within it?

That would explain why it seemed so uncomfortable and irritated.

The only way to find out more information was to go looking for another kodanos. It would mean another kill, but the possibility of an invasive species was a huge threat. This ecosystem was far more delicate than most people thought it was.

Leaving the kodanos behind, I ventured deeper into the forest. I must've moved off the Xathi warpath, for some of the lushness had returned. I took a deep breath, inhaling the rich aroma of the forest. By the time I felt the stalking vine wrap around my ankle, it was too late.

I was at its mercy as it yanked me off my feet and dragged me deeper into the forest.

ROKUL

General Rouhr insisted that I leave right away. Apparently, all of my routine duties would wait until the botanist was located.

I didn't even get a name or a physical description from anyone. As part of my punishment for honesty, the general told me to use my wits.

Takar didn't laugh. Out loud. Much.

I packed a few weapons and some basic gear.

And as Fen was fine-tuning the connection between the Aurora's A.I. and the Gateway, I'd need to take the trip the long way.

Probably for the best.

If I wasn't looking carefully, I would've missed Rigkon entirely. Thankfully, the forest's canopy wasn't as thick as it used to be. I could see the gap where trees had been cut down to make some kind of pathetic excuse for a road.

I landed my aerial unit as far away as I could from the squat row of buildings. From the look of them, one strong gust of wind could be their undoing. They were made of natural materials, likely harvested from the surrounding forest.

Vidia mentioned that this place was constructed as a jumping off point for rebuilding Fraga. If that project had been put on hold, why did these people remain? Surely, better houses were available. I thought of some of the makeshift settlements erected to house displaced refugees. Many of them weren't any better than the buildings before me. I retracted my previous thought.

I spied an open market with three stalls tended by two people. I powered off the aerial unit and jumped out, their eyes boring into me.

And now would come the ever-exciting game that seemed all the rage on Ankou now. Friendlies or anti-aliens?

Out here in the forest, I doubted they came across many Skotan. As far as I knew, none of the *Vengeance* crew had been stationed this far out. The strike teams operated in Nyheim unless otherwise instructed. The ground teams, much more numerous than the strike teams, were scattered through the human settlements and provided what aid they could.

Sometimes I wished I was part of a ground team. At least they had things to do other than busy work. Their work made a difference to people. The strike teams couldn't even handle a rogue plant.

I approached the open market. A large human female with a big round face smiled at me. From what I could see, she was missing most of her teeth. I took that to mean that this was an alien-friendly settlement.

"Well, we don't get your kind here very often. Are you here to deliver the support beams we ordered last week? My shop could really use it. It's right over there." She pointed at the building next to the market. "It has a little bit of everything. You can go in and have a look if you want."

"No, thank you. I'm not here about the beams, either." Her face fell a bit with disappointment but her smile remained.

"Oh," she said. "What can I do for you?"

"I'm looking for someone. A botanist. Dr. Briar." I explained. "They could've arrived anywhere within the last two days."

"A botanist?" the woman repeated. She looked to her companion, a rail-thin man who shrugged in response. "We've had one new person come by, but she didn't mention anything about being a botanist. She actually didn't talk much at all."

"I don't think that's who I'm looking for," I frowned.

Leena mentioned something about the botanist taking a field job. A botanist that worked in the field on this planet would often enter combat with the planet's vicious plant and animal life.

To me, that sounded like a job more suited for human males. Sure, Jeneva had lived out there, but I knew enough of her story to know she'd lived in the forest by necessity, not choice.

Since no one had given me a name or a description, I had to go with my gut.

"Are you sure the person you're looking for came through here?" the woman asked.

"That's what I was told," I replied.

"Perhaps you should try the Crooked Swiggen," she said brightly.

"What's a Crooked Swiggen?" I asked.

"It's our local watering hole, if you will," she giggled. "It's the only place to get food you don't have to cook yourself. Your botanist probably stopped in there for a drink and a bite."

"Right. Thank you for your help." The woman opened her mouth to say something else but I had already walked away. I wanted to find this botanist, get back to the general, and get on with things.

The building she indicated to was as unimpressive as the others, but there wasn't anything crooked about it.

The inside was so dark I needed a moment for my eyes to adjust.

There were only three people in this building. One tended the bar, one sat at the bar and the third was fast asleep at one of the tables. Everything was covered in dust and nothing looked nice.

I liked this place.

"I'm looking for a botanist. A Dr. Briar." I announced loudly enough for the male sleeping at the table to jolt awake.

The male sitting at the bar turned to face me. "I hired one, why?" he asked.

"My superior requires one. Turns out the one here was promised to us but decided to take a quick side job," I explained. "You're the side job?"

"Yeah," the male scratched his head. "We've been having some trouble with the local plant population."

"Where's Dr. Briar now?"

"Left a few hours ago. I'm getting a little worried, truth be told. Sun will go down in about an hour. The forest is a lot less hospitable in the dark," the male explained.

"It's not hospitable now," I grumbled.

"Exactly," he nodded.

"It would seem I'll be journeying into the forest," I sighed irritably.

"There's a supply store if you need anything." The

male gestured lazily in the general direction of the building on the other side of the market. In response, I pulled out the smaller of the two blasters I'd brought along.

"I think I'll be fine," I grinned. "Do you know which direction Dr. Briar went?"

"Nope." The male turned his attention back to his drink.

"Fantastic." I turned on my heel and stalked out of the bar. He was right, the light was already starting to fade. I needed to find this scientist quickly.

I looked at the ground for any disturbances. It was too covered in leaves and other bits discarded by the forest to show footprints, but that was merely an obstacle. There weren't any outlying footprints on the thin road, so the botanist must've gone into the forest straight from the bar.

I took an educated guess and headed into the woods. I soon found a faint trail of compressed debris and broken twigs. Something had come through within the last few hours. I hoped it was Dr. Briar, but, in this forest, there was never any guarantees.

When we still lived aboard the *Vengeance*, we routinely ran night patrols. The forest surrounding the *Vengeance* lit up with something I'd learned was called bioluminescence. Apparently, little colonies of glowing bacteria lived on the plants and trees.

I wasn't much of a one for scenery, but the glowing forest had been a sight to behold.

Who knew tiny bugs would be pretty?

As I walked through this section of the forest, I found myself disappointed. As the light faded, the bioluminescent bacteria colonies began to glow, but it was dim and faded compared to what I remembered.

Many of the trees bore signs of damage. I assumed the Xathi tore through here on their way to destroy Fraga.

Something hard, harder than a branch, crunched underfoot. I took a step back and looked down. It was part of a Xathi leg. Rage boiled up inside me and my lip curled in disgust. With one swift motion, I picked up the Xathi leg and lobbed it as hard as I could against the nearest tree. It shattered into pieces.

I didn't feel any better.

I'd accepted the fact that return to my home system was likely impossible, but that didn't mean I wasn't angry about everything the Xathi had taken from me.

All of us were angry and it would take a long time for that fury to fade away. For many of us, not just the *Vengeance* crew but the humans, too, that resentment would mar us for the rest of our lives.

I moved on, deeper into the forest. The trail wasn't as strong now and it hadn't been strong to begin with. At one point, I thought I'd lost it completely, but then I stumbled onto a piece of compelling evidence that someone – or something – had come through recently.

A few meters in front of me was the body of a sentient tree. It wasn't a sorvuc. I'd dealt with enough of them to feel confident identifying them. It must've been the other species. Its named slipped my mind.

Whatever it was, it'd been badly torn up. Its lower leg was completely torn off. Dark, sticky sap pooled at the break. Stranger still, the creature lay face down. Its back had been split clean open.

If this was the work of the botanist, he was a fearsome warrior indeed.

Now I felt excited to meet him. Perhaps his counsel would be beneficial to us. He certainly knew how to kill sentient plants.

Of course, there was the possibility that something other than the botanist had done this. That just made me more excited. At least that scenario promised a good fight.

It'd been weeks since I'd had a good fight. Not a good position for a combat soldier to be in.

I left the dead creature behind and continued my search. The light was fading fast. Within ten minutes it was too dark to see the trail I'd been following. I wasn't worried about losing my way. I had a navigation system tapped into the *Aurora's* network based on Karzin's satellite system that he had set up in his quest to find a way home. It would work even all the way out here.

The human male in the Crooked Swiggen had had a point when he said the forest becomes even less hospitable after dark. Despite my weapons, walking through a forest like this in the dark with no backup was not a tempting prospect.

If the botanist did kill that sentient plant, I reasoned he'd be able to take care of himself out here in the dark. I couldn't afford to waste any more time. I'd done what General Rouhr asked.

Just as I turned around to make my way back, an ear-splitting scream echoed through the forest.

A female's scream.

TELLA

The Helmria Ithalma was a rare flower. Only three or four of them had ever been found.

Their vibrant petals were extremely sensitive to sunlight, so sensitive that even the thick layer of leaves and branches that made up the forest canopy didn't provide enough protection.

Luckily for the Helmria Ithalma, it figured out another option. Occasionally, if the topography was correct and the timing was perfect, the seed of a Helmria would take root in a shallow cave. The trick was, the cave couldn't be too shallow. Any shallower than ten, maybe twelve, feet and the Helmria would wither away and die.

Just because the Helmria Ithalma stayed rooted where it was planted didn't mean it was non-sentient.

Since it didn't have the luxury of mobility like the kodanos or the sorvuc, the Helmria had had to get creative in terms of finding food.

It was a carnivorous flower that required a considerable amount of food per day to survive. Remarkably, the Helmria had evolved vines that it could move at will. No one knew how many vines a single Helmria could grow, nor did anyone know how far a single vine could reach.

The forests of Ankou were ribboned with vines that seemed to have a mind of their own. There was a theory that every sentient vine in the forests actually belonged to the elusive Helmria. I wasn't sure about that. But I did have some idea of how many vines a single Helmria could produce. The leading experts were way off.

And how did I come across such a groundbreaking piece of information?

Well, as it happened, I was hanging by my ankles in the dank lair of an angry, starving Helmria Ithalma.

It had at least twenty vines, though most of them were coiled up underneath the brilliant bloom. I guessed it was to conserve energy. This forest could no longer support the voracious appetite of a Helmria.

Its vibrant crimson petals splayed apart to reveal a cruel, circular mouth-like hole lined with needle-like teeth in the center of the flower. For the better part of an hour, the Helmria had been trying to turn me into lunch.

"I don't want to do this to you!" I shouted angrily as I sliced through another vine. With only a small handful of known specimens, I wanted to escape its clutches without damaging it too severely.

When I got out of here, the first thing I planned on doing was reporting this to the Ankou Botany Board. I wasn't sure if it was still functioning after the Xathi invasion, but it would resurrect itself for a Helmria.

I'd already cataloged its exact location. I'd pulled out my datapad and jotted everything down while fending off the probing vines. It was thanks to that momentary, but incredibly important, distraction, that I had a gash on my calf.

Apparently, the damp coating on the outside of a Helmria hurt like a bitch when it came into contact with a cut.

Trust me on that.

The Helmria launched another vine attack towards me. I defected it with a flick of my hunting knife. I didn't slice through the threatening vine. I only nicked it. The Helmria hissed and spat.

I assumed that was a reaction to pain or frustration. I wasn't sure if it could feel pain. I hoped it couldn't. I felt bad enough about damaging it. I didn't want to make it even more aggressive.

But if it could, what an interesting result!

Another vine lashed at me before I was prepared to deflect it. It wrapped around my wrist and squeezed until I was forced to drop my knife. It landed point down in the middle of another thick vine. The Helmria flailed about.

"See, I bet you regret doing that," I scolded it. "You've only gone and hurt yourself more. I bet that vine's useless to you now."

My knife was my most prized possession. However, it wasn't my only weapon. I pulled a small blaster out of the holster around my waist. I didn't like to use it. I was a fair shot, but I wasn't as good with it as I was with my knife.

Another vine came at me. I fired a small beam that pierced the vine through. The Helmria wailed and thrashed.

"Give me back my knife and I won't do that again. Does that sound fair to you?" I groaned. The Helmria responded by lashing out with a vine.

This time, I shot a piece of it clean off. For a brief moment, I got a perfect view of the exposed nerves that ran through the vine. Fascinating. I wish I brought more supplies for collecting samples. Every lab in the settled areas would beg to have me on their team.

"You and I could make a great team. Do you not

realize this?" I yelled at the stupid plant. "I'd let you live! You could even be my pet! I'd be open to that!"

It swiped at me again. I fired the blaster and missed, but the noise startled it enough to make it yank the vine away.

"Good! You're learning," I said. It still had me suspended by my ankles. I guessed that the only reason it didn't lower me right into its gaping maw was that I was too big. Its mouth was big enough to swallow my head, but there was no way in hell that it could swallow my shoulders. Now that my knife was out of reach, I was tempted to shoot myself down. I took my eyes off the Helmria for a split second to look at the ground beneath me. It was covered in vines. From that brief glance, I couldn't tell if they were living or not. I didn't want to find out the hard way.

Another vine came at me. I fired. Nothing happened. My little blaster was out of ammo.

"Damn it!" I screamed. When the next vine came for me, I had no choice but to grab it with my bare hands. It felt like solid muscle as it struggled against my grip. I dug my nails into its thick skin in an attempt to cause pain.

It wasn't working. Something to note.

I was out of options, but I wasn't going to give in that easily. If this thing wanted to eat me, it was going

to have to work harder than it had ever worked in its
life.

I kicked my legs, trying to break free of the grip the
Helmria Ithalma had on my ankles, but it was no use.
My ankles might as well have been encased in cement.

Then I heard something that made me pause. It
sounded like thumping coming from somewhere above
me. This particular Helmria didn't live in a typical cave.
The opening to its lair was above me, made from a
lattice of dead roots. I could still see the hole it dragged
me through. My arms were covered in shallow scrapes
as a result.

The thumping turned into a cracking sound. I
craned my neck and looked up just in time to see a
thick red arm punch through the opening of the
Helmria lair. Soon after, a huge scaly Skotan dropped
down onto the floor, weapons drawn. He fired like
lightning at every vine near him before shooting at the
vines that held me. I fell unceremoniously to the
ground and landed hard.

"Son of a bitch!" I hissed. I reached for my knife, but
the Skotan grabbed it first.

"I've got this," he said. Then he winked.

Who the hell did he think he was?

With my knife in hand, he rushed at the bloom of
the Helmria.

"Wait!" I shouted but it was too late.

He drove my knife deep into its gaping mouth.

Dammit.

It let out a high-pitched whine that sounded like a scream. Its petals twitched and its vines thrashed. When the Skotan removed the blade, its petals closed up and the vines went still.

"This yours?" the Skotan asked, holding up my knife. It was covered in green liquid sap. I silently took it from him and sheathed it without cleaning it. That sap could provide valuable information later on.

"You're welcome," the Skotan leaned in to whisper to me.

"What exactly am I thanking you for? For killing an incredibly rare species of sentient flower?" I asked.

"For saving your life," he grinned. I took a moment to look him over.

He was handsome and fully aware of it, and also armed to the teeth.

"Do you always walk around dying forests looking for a fight?" I jutted my chin at his many weapons. "You just killed an incredibly rare and very endangered plant!"

The alien looked at me as if I had turned into a plant myself.

"It's lucky for you I was out here," he said. "If I hadn't been looking for a botanist, I wouldn't have heard you scream."

"A botanist?" I blinked.

"Yeah, they're like gardeners, but with more science. Did you see anyone else out here before you were grabbed by that thing?"

Handsome, yet dense.

Terrible combination.

"I'm the botanist. Why are you looking for me?" I demanded.

"You're Dr. Briar?" Now he was the one who looked surprised. "You're not a man?"

"Last time I checked, I wasn't," I replied, glancing down at my chest. Yup. Still there.

To his credit, he got past the woman thing pretty quickly.

"You remember your friend Leena? The one you blew off today in favor of tangling with a death plant?" he asked.

"I didn't mean to blow her off," I said quickly. "Did she send you to fetch me?"

"My general did," the Skotan said. "I'm not allowed back on duty until I bring you to the capital."

"Wow. Did you piss him off or something?" I folded my arms across my chest.

His face fell a bit. "Yes, I did."

Handsome and dense, but also honest. Less of a terrible combination.

Slightly.

"Right. Well, we better get back, then." Leaving the remains of the poor Helmria Ithalma behind, I climbed the lifeless vines and wiggled through the opening. The Skotan followed behind.

"You're not going to thank me for saving you?" the Skotan asked.

"Thank you," I said. "Now, let's get back to Rigkon. This botanist needs a drink."

ROKUL

I'd like to think I was a hard person to surprise after everything I've seen and done. This botanist surprised me.

I mean, yeah, the woman thing, but whatever.

What surprised me more was the fact that she didn't appear at all fazed by her near-death experience.

Apparently, I didn't understand the botany profession as well as I thought I did.

I walked several yards behind her as she stalked through the forest with natural ease. That was just as surprising as her casual reaction to the carnivorous plant.

I'd saved her life, yet she was annoyed with me for killing the horrid thing.

And she was really pretty.

Lots of surprises.

"Slow down!" I called. I could've moved faster if I wanted to but frankly, I didn't want to. I'd had a long day, I fought a plant, and I wasn't in the mood to break a sweat anymore. I was still annoyed that I'd been sent on this mission as a form of punishment.

"Catch up!" she called back. I couldn't help but smile just a little. The girl had some bite to her, no doubt about it.

This was much better than toting a pale, skinny scientist-type through the forest. I didn't have to worry about being her bodyguard. With a shake of my head, I jogged to catch up with her.

"You never told me your name," I said.

"Dr. Briar," she shot back.

"I can't keep calling you that. I rescued you. We should at least be friends," I grinned. "Tell me yours, I'll tell you mine?"

She turned her head to face me and gave me a long once over. I wasn't sure what she was looking for, but she found it.

"Fine," she smiled. "I'm Tella."

"Rokul," I replied. "I'm a-"

"Skotan. Yes, I know," she said. "I made a point to learn about the aliens that saved our planet."

"Did you?" I was impressed. Not many humans went out of their way to learn about us. "Any thoughts?"

"Not particularly," she replied. "After seeing the Xathi, it's hard to see you and the other aliens as shocking."

"Not much surprises you," I ventured.

"Almost nothing. Finding that Helmria Ithalma was a surprise, but not for the reasons you're probably thinking," she replied. "They're incredibly rare. I wouldn't be surprised if the Xathi killed most of them as they destroyed the human settlements."

"From where I stood, wiping those things out might be a good thing," I commented. Tella bit the inside of her cheek, I suspect to stop the frown tugging at the corner of her mouth.

Even though it was dark, Tella didn't seem lost. I checked my navigation often just to make sure we were going in the right direction, which we were.

I wasn't sure what time it was when we got back to Rigkon, but I was more than ready to go back to the capital. I started off toward my aerial unit.

Tella started off toward the Crooked Swiggen.

"Where are you going?" I asked. "We have to report to my superior as soon as possible."

"I told you, I need a drink," she said without looking back. She pushed her way into the squat, dirty building and disappeared. I looked between the door and my aerial unit a few times before letting out a long groan.

"One drink and we're out of here," I muttered to

myself as I stalked through the door of the Crooked Swiggen.

Tella had already made herself at home, standing by the center table. She shrugged off her gear pack and the thigh-length earth-green jacket she wore, revealing the gray thin-strapped top beneath.

The first clear look I had of her struck me and, without even meaning to, I took a moment to admire her long, lean body.

Her curves were another surprise, another nice one. A very nice one. And then I noticed something else.

In the low light, they were almost impossible to see, but her arms were covered in scars in all shapes and sizes. For her small stature, she was certainly tougher than she looked. Her scars reminded me of mine.

Battle scars.

That explained why she was so unfazed by her encounter with the carnivorous flower.

By the time I joined Tella at the table, the barkeep had already placed a drink in front of her. She picked it up and downed it in one gulp. She set the drink down with a hard thump and signaled for another one.

"Oh, no," I warned her. "You've had your drink. It's time to go."

"I almost died. Let a girl have a few drinks," she said dismissively. When the barkeep came back, he had two drinks. One for Tella and one for me.

"What the skrell," I shrugged and downed my drink right along with her. She wasn't the only one who'd had a bad day.

"That's more like it," she grinned. Her eyes were shining and her movements were looser. I hadn't observed human inebriation often, but those were two of the most consistent symptoms. I wondered if Tella would start dancing wildly, crying uncontrollably, or just fall asleep. Those were other common symptoms I'd seen.

I decided none of those things would be appropriate for Tella.

"That's it," I said firmly. "We're leaving now."

"I haven't gotten paid yet." Tella shook her head.

"What?"

"I was hired to come out here," she said. "I'm not leaving until I get paid for the work I've done."

"You did the work before receiving payment?" I groaned. "I thought you were a professional."

"I got half up front," she said defensively. "It's not my first time doing this, you know? But I need the rest."

"Who needs to pay you?" I asked.

"The project foreman. A man named Gille," she replied.

"Foreman? What project is happening here?" I asked. As far as I knew, the rebuilding of Fraga was delayed until further notice.

"I think the people here are still hopeful that Fraga will be rebuilt sooner rather than later," Tella reasoned. "I can't think of any other reason why someone would choose to live out here."

"Where can we find Gille? We need to get you back to Nyheim so I can get off probation," I said.

"Oh," she said with a knowing grin. "That's right. I forgot you were in deep trouble with your betters."

"General Rouhr isn't my better, and I'm not in deep trouble. I'm in standard trouble," I explained.

"So, this sort of punishment assignment is normal for you?" she queried, lifting her brows.

"Not that it's any of your business, but," I scrubbed my hand through my short hair, "it's not uncommon for me to run my mouth," I admitted.

"Somehow, I don't have a hard time imagining that," Tella giggled as she took a sip of the fresh drink the bartender had procured for her.

"You're a real charmer," I sighed.

"I know," she beamed. "Complimenting me won't get me out of this bar and into your little space ship. I'm not leaving without my money."

"Fine," I groaned. "Where is he?"

"How the hell should I know?"

"I understand that you don't want to make my life easier. You don't know me. But can you please try not to make my life any harder?" I gave her a sharp smile.

"I spent the better part of an hour suspended over a mouth full of teeth," she replied. "And then I lost the incredibly rare sample. I think I've had the worse day. Since he's not here, Gille's probably crashed back at wherever he sleeps."

"Which is where?" I pushed.

Tella lifted a finger, indicating for me to be silent while she took another sip of her drink. I rolled my eyes. This slight, scar-covered botanist was quickly becoming a pain in my ass, which I believed was the proper description, if I had learned correctly from Leena.

"I've only met the guy once. I don't make a habit of learning where strange men sleep," she replied. "We'll simply have to find him in the morning. I'm sure he'll be at the same barstool he was at today. There's not a lot of places to go in Rigkon, in case you didn't notice."

"I noticed," I grumbled. "Excuse me, I must call my superior."

"Calling for backup?" She giggled as I stood up from the table.

"Something like that," I muttered as I walked out of the Crooked Swiggen. I took out my comm unit and reached out to General Rouhr.

"I expected you back hours ago," he said when he answered.

"So did I, sir. I spent hours in the forest searching for the botanist," I reported.

"Well, where is she?" General Rouhr demanded. For a brief moment, I considered lying and telling the general that I hadn't found the botanist, but I wisely decided against it.

"At the moment, she's getting drunk," I replied.

"What?" General Rouhr barked.

"She's out here on a job and she refuses to leave until she's been paid. She's had a few drinks while waiting," I explained.

"Perfect," General Rouhr sighed. "She'll be in no condition to travel in an aerial unit. Find a place to sleep. Stay there for the night. Make sure she gets enough rest. If we're lucky, she'll have a busy day tomorrow."

"Yes, sir."

General Rouhr disconnected.

This wasn't the outcome I wanted.

I walked back into the Crooked Swiggen. Tella had moved on to her fourth drink.

"We're staying here for the night," I told her. Her upper lip curled up involuntarily. At least we felt the same way about this place.

I walked past the table and went straight for the bar.

"We need beds for the night," I told the barkeep.

"Guesthouse is down the road," he grunted in response.

"I'll have another of what she's having." I gestured to Tella. The barkeep just nodded.

With a fresh drink in hand, I sauntered over to Tella's table and took a seat. If I was going to be stuck here for a night, I was going to enjoy it.

"You look less disgruntled," Tella observed.

"Oh, I'm still disgruntled," I corrected her. "But now I'm disgruntled with a drink in my hand."

"That makes two of us," Tella grinned, her smile lighting up the dim room.

I smiled back and took a long sip of my drink.

TELLA

If I were in a real bar, after six drinks I'd be unconscious, if not sick to my stomach.

But the Crooked Swiggen watered their drinks down, probably to make their bottles last longer. By my calculation, I'd consumed the equivalent of two normal drinks and I was nowhere near as drunk as I wanted to be.

I signaled Swiggy behind the bar for another drink. He obliged.

Even though I knew the drinks were watered down, old Swiggen charged as much as a bar in the capital city would. I wanted to call him on it, but I feared he would cut me off and that would be far worse.

I was going to blow the first half of my payment at this grimy hole in the wall.

Dammit.

At least the company was good.

In addition to being handsome, dense, and honest, Rokul also had a decent sense of humor. Now that he'd had a few drinks in him as well, he was less of an ass.

"I still don't understand what you do!" he exclaimed. "I thought botanists grew plants and then looked at their plants under a microscope to learn how to grow better plants! That's what botanists do on my home planet."

"You have botanists on your planet?" I asked.

"It has a different name but it's basically the same job," he explained. His skin looked like fire in the low yellow light of the Crooked Swiggen. "However, we don't have sentient plants."

"That's where the big difference is," I explained. "I can do all the other stuff you mentioned. I used to have a wonderful garden before those crystal bug bastards arrived. I was the top botanist at my lab, too."

"Top botanist?" Rokul laughed. "What an honor."

I reached across the table to shove his shoulder. The moment I touched his skin, I felt a strange flip in my stomach.

Rokul's shoulder was all muscle. And the skin was like nothing I'd ever felt before. Before I gave into the urge to stroke his arm, I pulled away quickly.

"It was an honor," I said defensively. "A large part of

botany is fieldwork. A large part of fieldwork here is plants that want to rip you apart."

"Hence the weapons," he nodded. "I noticed you're fond of your knife."

"Family heirloom," I grinned. "And it's satisfying to slash things with."

"You're more soldier than scientist." Rokul folded his muscular arms across his equally muscular chest.

I didn't know what his vest was made of, but it left nothing to the imagination. I averted my gaze before he caught me starting. I didn't need his head getting any bigger.

"I guess I am," I nodded looking into the shallow depth of my drink. I couldn't believe I'd already gone through another drink and I still didn't feel any different. Screw the wrath of Swiggen, I wanted a real drink.

"Swiggy!" I called. The barkeeper looked up but didn't realize it was him that I was speaking to until I waved my hand. He sucked in a breath, threw a dingy towel over his shoulder, and approached the table.

"Can I help you?"

"Can I ask to change the water-to-spirit percentage in my drinks?" I asked.

"Excuse me?" His brows shot up.

"I'm not a lightweight or anything. But if I can have six of these and feel nothing, either I have a serious problem or you're watering down my drinks," I said.

Rokul looked taken aback. So did Swiggen.

"I have to make stock last or I go under," Swiggen muttered. I'd suspected that might be the case but I hadn't thought he'd actually admit it.

"I'll tell you what," I leaned in like I was going to tell him a secret. "Give us a bottle. It can be your lowest-quality bottle. It doesn't matter, as long as it's pure. I'll pay the price of a full top-quality bottle."

"Deal." Swiggen grinned and returned to his place behind the bar.

"You really like to drink, don't you?" Rokul chuckled.

"Technically, we haven't started drinking yet," I reminded him. "Right now, we're more well-hydrated than anything."

"There are worse things to be," Rokul grinned. "Though I'd also like a real drink."

"That's the spirit," I grinned. At the same moment, Swiggen came back and placed a dark brown bottle half filled with liquid on the table.

"No, that's the spirit," Rokul pointed at the bottle. I tipped my head back and laughed, aware that it was the loudest sound in the room.

"That was stupid," I giggled.

"Yet you laughed," Rokul pointed out. He poured us

each half a glass of clear liquid that smelled so strongly it made my nose wrinkle.

"Maybe I like stupid things," I shrugged and took a small sip. I winced as the spirits slid down my throat. "I know why this is the lowest quality," I shuddered.

Rokul took a sip for himself but didn't react.

"It tastes fine," he said.

"Clearly my taste buds are different than your Skotan taste buds." I held my breath as I took another sip. Already, I started to feel the warm feeling I wanted. A little more and I wouldn't be able to think straight and I wouldn't be able to think about...them.

I shook my head violently as if I could shake away the bad memories.

"Are you well?" Rokul asked.

"Yes," I said too brightly. I forced myself to take a longer sip this time, even though it burned going down. "Just trying to shake the horrible taste out of my mouth."

"Maybe you should've stuck to the watered-down drinks," Rokul said in a condescending tone that made me want to pour his drink over his head.

"No way in hell." Against my better judgment, I drained the rest of my drink and poured myself another, which was no easy task. I now saw two cups where there had only been one.

"Bring it on," Rokul challenged. He downed his own cup.

"Is it a competition now?" I arched my brow and smirked.

"Isn't it always?" he asked.

"You mean drinking or just life in general?" I replied.

"Both." He poured himself another drink. "Tell me about your scars."

"Excuse me?" I sputtered.

"That one on your shoulder. I have one that looks just like it. What's it from?" He pointed to a scar that had an odd curved shape. He brought his finger over and ran it over my scar.

I shuddered in pleasure. His touch set off sparks that spiraled through me, straight to my core. "Nasty encounter with a lone Luurizi," I replied, voice carefully neutral. "He didn't get me with the spikes on his hoofs, but I didn't escape the corkscrew horn."

"That's how I got mine!" he grinned. "It was a few days after we crash landed and I thought the Luurizi would make for some good meals."

While he took a sip of his drink, I surveyed his arms. I didn't want to ask about the nastiest of the scars. Usually, scars like that came with sad stories.

I didn't want to hear any sad stories tonight. Then I

saw another interesting scar. It was almost a perfect half circle, with uniform ridges.

"What happened there?" I asked pointing to the inside of his right forearm before tracing it with my finger.

Nope, that wasn't the alcohol making me do that. It was pure, simple, good ol' fashioned desire.

The kind I planned to stuff to the side, really quickly.

Even if he was handsome. And honest. And made me laugh.

"I got that from a Xezleq," he said.

"I can't even pronounce what you just said," I snorted.

"Humans can't," he replied. "It's like one of those vines, but with way more legs. And also a dorsal spine. And eyes all over its body."

"So, nothing like a vine, at all," I laughed.

"I guess not," Rokul chuckled.

By the time we finished the bottle, Swiggen was practically pushing us out of his bar.

"See you tomorrow, Swiggen!" I called. He didn't answer me. No fun at all.

"Where's the guesthouse?" Rokul asked.

"It's the building that's not the Crooked Swiggen or the supply shop. You could've figured that one out. There's not that many buildings here," I said.

"Count them," Rokul challenged.

I scoffed as I tried to focus on the buildings, but as soon as I did, they blurred together and the world wouldn't stay straight.

"Too hard. Next question," I giggled.

"Come on." Rokul laughed and tugged me along. Unfortunately, the unpaved roads and my drunken state did not mix. My foot caught on a divot and I fell face first into the dirt. It might've hurt, but I couldn't tell, I was laughing too hard.

"Graceful," Rokul leaned over me and laughed. "Come on, let's get you up."

Apparently, he was drunker than he'd let on, because he lost his balance and fell to the ground beside me.

"Graceful," I smirked. I rolled over to face him but somehow, I ended up half on top of him. His hand was on my lower back. We were laughing together, making half-assed attempts to get back on our feet. I wasn't sure if he pulled me or if I moved myself, but now I was fully on top of him.

"You're making it worse," I giggled.

"Am I?"

Suddenly his eyes were the only thing in focus. I'd never seen such intense eyes.

Somehow this felt right. I could stay like this forever.

Before I knew what I was doing, I leaned down and kissed him. His hand found its way to the base of my neck. He held me to him while he kissed me deeper, teasing, tasting. Our tongues danced together as my chest pressed against his.

I shifted so my legs were on either side of him. As I lost myself in his kiss, my hips began to rock and sway. A soft groan escaped his lips between kisses. His hands travelled to my hips, grinding me into him. Beneath me, I felt him grow hard. Desire shot through my body, igniting me all the way to my core. I reached beneath me and pressed my palm into the base of his length. He groaned again.

Somewhere behind us, a door slammed. The spell broke.

We were in the middle of a dirt road, drunk and groping each other.

This wasn't right.

"We should get to the guesthouse," I said quickly, rolling to the side.

"Yes," Rokul helped me to my feet. "Apparently, you have a big day ahead of you."

ROKUL

I woke up on the floor.

I did not fall asleep on the floor, so my confusion was understandable.

In the cot next to me, Tella had managed to stay in her bed through the night. Her hair was a tangled mess that covered her face, but she looked more comfortable than I felt.

Beyond her, the other two cots in the one-room guesthouse were unoccupied, but had clearly been slept in.

"Tella," I muttered.

She only groaned in response. "Tella." I lifted my upper body up so I could tap her on the arm.

General Rouhr had probably expected me in his

office at sunrise. At this rate, I'd be doing punishment missions until I retired.

"Go away," she moaned.

"I can't go away," I chuckled. "It's time to get up."

"No, it isn't," she insisted.

I struggled to my feet, trying to ignore how heavy my tongue felt and the pounding behind my temples.

I don't know what we drank last night, but I definitely underestimated the power of the Crooked Swiggen. I needed to find out what I'd drunk so I could keep a few bottles on hand at home.

Tella still hadn't moved.

With a sigh, I reached out to push her shoulder or pull her hand, I wasn't sure which. The more I thought about it, I wasn't sure how to touch her at all. My hand froze just an inch away from her skin.

Fragmented images of the night before flitted through my mind's eye. I perfectly remembered the taste of her lips and the softness of her body, how she'd felt pressed against me. The memory of it alone caused a stir in me.

I looked away from her for a few moments to quiet my mind. When I looked back at Tella, her eyes were open and she was staring at me.

"You okay?" She looked concerned.

"Yeah. Just the effects of the drink," I said quickly.

Tella laughed.

"I should've stuck to the watered-down bottles," she groaned. She extended her hand. "Help me up."

I took her hand and pulled her out of bed. I must've pulled her too quickly, for when she stood on her own two feet, she swayed and looked disoriented. I held her shoulders until she stabilized herself.

Tella blinked and shook her head as if she could shake away the negative side effects of last night. When she opened her eyes to look at me, she paused. She bit her bottom lip like she was contemplating something.

"About last night," she began.

"We should talk about that," I added.

"We're going to be colleagues now, aren't we?" she asked. I nodded. "Maybe we should chalk it up to a night of bad judgment and loose morals and leave it at that."

"I think that's the wisest course of action."

Her suggestion was a reasonable one. There was a serious job to do and any kind of relationship outside of professional parameters could prove to be a distraction.

I almost laughed at myself. I sounded just like my brother.

Not really a surprise. Half of my thoughts were essentially his, since he'd spent so much of our lives lecturing me about my impulsiveness.

Hard to believe I was the older brother.

It was a shame that my mind called upon Takar's reasoning at this moment.

Tella was lovely and there was no doubt that I was attracted to her.

Not just physically, either. She was bright, clever, and one of the toughest human females I'd ever encountered. I wasn't worried about how she'd fare with General Rouhr, Karzin, and the rest of the strike team.

A professional relationship was not at all what I wanted.

"Great," she smiled tightly. "Now that that's settled, shall we go?"

"Are you sure you don't want to spend another night in luxury?" I gestured to the rickety beds and threadbare blankets.

Tella made a sound halfway between a laugh and a scoff before turning on her heel and sauntering out of the guesthouse.

"I'll take that as a no?" I called after her. I checked our beds once more to ensure nothing was left behind before following her out. She stood near the market, waiting for me.

"Fancy one for the road?" She jerked her thumb in the direction of the Crooked Swiggen.

"No, thank you," I laughed.

"Me, either. But I still have to get my payment. I'm

willing to bet Gille is already at his stool." She waited for me and together we walked back into the dark establishment.

"There's my favorite customers!" The barkeeper greeted us enthusiastically. "Fancy another bottle?"

"No offense, Swiggy. But I'd rather die," Tella replied. Swiggen, or whatever his name really was, chuckled and went back to minding his bar.

Tella approached the single male sitting on a barstool.

"I'm here for the rest of my payment, Gille," Tella told him.

"Have you cleared the forest of pests?" the male replied.

"You didn't ask me to clear the forest of pests." She placed her hands on her hips. "You asked me to take care of one rogue kodanos."

"I've seen at least five of them," Gille replied. "If you've only killed one, then the job's not done."

"I didn't see signs of any others," Tella argued. "I did my job. You said there was only one kodanos that needed to be investigated. Pay up!"

"I don't think so," Gille smirked.

"Excuse me?" Tella demanded.

Gille turned his back to her, refusing to acknowledge her. His blatant dismissal of her made my blood boil but I contained myself. As much as I wanted to ram his forehead into the bar, I wanted to see how Tella would handle it more.

I wasn't disappointed. She grabbed him by the back of his shirt and yanked. She wasn't quite strong enough to pull him off his seat, but she got his attention.

"I want my payment," she hissed. She placed one hand on the pommel of her hunting knife in Gille's sight. He narrowed his eyes and, before Tella could react, he grabbed her wrist and shoved her back.

Before she could square up again, I stepped in. Now I was the one to grab Gille by the back of his shirt and I was certainly strong enough to pull him from his seat. He took one look at me and all the color drained from his face.

"Haven't spent much time around Skotans, have you?" I smiled. It was almost my polite one. "We're actually sticklers for rules, agreements, contracts. Pay the nice lady or else you're going to get to know me a lot better than you want to." Without looking away from me, Gille reached into his pocket and slid a datapad across the floor to Tella.

"Transfer the payment," he instructed her, then to me he said, "See? I can be reasonable."

"We'll see," I replied coldly.

"I transferred the payment and a little tip for my troubles," Tella stared dead-eyed as she gave the datapad back to Gille. "Call it a PITA tax, pain in the ass."

Good. I did get that expression right.

I released my grip on the human male's shirt. He was smart enough to stay quiet as he got back onto his seat at the bar.

"Ready?" I asked Tella. She nodded.

"Bye, Swiggen!" Tella called to our bar-keeper friend. Swiggen nodded his goodbyes.

Once Tella and I were out of earshot, I turned to her.

"I still haven't adjusted to the inferiority of human males," I said.

Tella laughed.

"Some of them aren't so bad. Swiggen was all right. Though I can understand how every human male looks inferior compared to you." She clamped her lips shut.

I didn't know how to respond. I could've easily interpreted her remark as flirtatious and I wanted to flirt back, however, we'd both agreed to remain professional while we worked together.

This was confusing. I didn't like confusing. But I did like her.

Skrell.

"Tell me more about what's been happening," Tella said quickly. We arrived at my aerial unit. I helped her step up into the passenger seat, then walked around to the pilot's seat.

"We found a giant sentient plant living underground out in the desert," I explained as I powered up the unit.

"Oh, is that all?" I knew Tella meant it as a joke, but she had no idea what she was in for.

"No," I replied. "It's been attacking settlements and cities. No one's sure how. The plant secretes a memory-erasing gas or something like that."

"I now realize why you've gone to the trouble of hunting me down," Tella said quietly.

"Dr. Leena Dewitt recommended you," I replied. "She said you are the best of the best."

"She's not wrong," Tella agreed. "Gosh, I haven't seen Leena in years."

"I'm sure you'll get a chance to catch up," I said. "General Rouhr will fill you in on the situation in more detail, but the short of it is that we're dealing with something no one can figure out. We need you to help us."

"No pressure," Tella laughed nervously.

"I think you can handle it," I grinned.

TELLA

When Rokul and I arrived in Nyheim, he took me straight to General Rouhr. General Rouhr was polite, but didn't give me the briefing Rokul had led me to believe I'd receive.

Instead, he immediately passed me on to Leena, and Rokul and I parted ways. He had to speak to General Rouhr about something, probably about getting off probation.

He told me he'd see me later. I couldn't decide if the prospect made me excited or nervous.

Someone else, a Valorni who didn't introduce himself, escorted me to the building's lab, where I assumed Leena would be waiting for me. She was in the lab, but she clearly wasn't expecting me. She was in the middle of recording data.

When I entered, she motioned for me to wait. While she took notes and squinted at the lines of data on her console, I took a moment to familiarize myself with the lab. It wasn't as nice as the one Leena and I used to work in at the university, but after the Xathi invasion, I knew we were lucky to have as much as we did.

"I wasn't told you'd be arriving today," Leena said as a way of letting me know she was ready to talk. "Then again, you were supposed to be here days ago."

"I apologize," I said. "I took a job in the field that took much longer to complete than I anticipated, especially since the guy refused to pay me, and-"

"I don't care," Leena grinned. "You're here now. So, can we get to work please?"

I remembered that about Leena. Many words could be used to describe her, but friendly was never the first one that came to mind.

We weren't exactly friends when we used to share a lab. Our stations were positioned next to each other and we often talked to each other because we both felt that everyone else in our lab was a complete moron.

We made small talk and took our breaks together, but we never socialized with each other outside of the lab. Both of us preferred it that way. We were each other's best option at the time.

"Yes. But I found something odd with one of the kodanos," I tried to explain, but Leena cut me off again.

"We have bigger plant problems than that," she said briskly. "Have you been briefed yet?"

"Not really," I replied. "General Rouhr said you'd fill me in." Apparently, that wasn't the answer Leena wanted to hear. She sucked in her cheeks. I could tell she was trying to control her temper, something I'd never seen Leena attempt to do. It looked like she'd softened up a bit in the last few years.

"When the remains of the Xathi ship crashed back down into the surface of our planet, it made a considerable impact," Leena began. "From what we understand, it appears that our actions have disturbed an ancient species of sentient plant that no one has ever seen before."

"What does it look like?" I asked.

"That's the thing," Leena continued. "No one has seen it. One of our colleagues, Annie Parker, is a geologist. She and Karzin, one of Rouhr's men, discovered the damn thing while they were rappelling into a crater. That crater turned out to be its home. It attacked them. It almost killed them twice, but they never got a good look at it. We think it's been attacking other places, too."

"Rokul mentioned something about that," I nodded. "He said it can alter memories?"

"It released an unusual airborne chemical that can suppress memory," Leena replied. "I made an antidote of sorts to stop the continuing effects of the chemical, but I haven't been able to retrieve lost memories. All we know is that this plant can reach the cities. I think it sends out vines, but instead of like the ones in the forest, they travel underground until they erupt.

"The only trace it leaves behind, besides damage and dead bodies, is perfectly circular craters in the earth. They're exact miniatures of the crater we think the thing lives in. That crater is huge. Half a mile across."

"This plant is gigantic then," I replied. "If people have been dying, why isn't this more well-known?"

"General Rouhr thought it best to keep everything under wraps until we know more," Leena explained. "After the Xathi, the last thing we need is for everyone to panic again. The people in the places that have been attacked know that something happened, but they don't know what. And until we know for sure, we don't want to tell them anything that could be just more misinformation."

"That's sad," I frowned. "Those poor people must be jumping at shadows."

"Maybe if you'd gotten here sooner, we would've found a solution by now." Leena's smile looked sweet at first glance, but I could see the venom in her expression.

If memory served, Leena had a sister who was the

nicest person on the planet. What I wouldn't give to work with her instead.

"Do any of your alien friends have a time machine?" I snapped. "If so, I'll happily go back and decline that job. In the likely event that they don't possess that technology, I don't know what you expect me to do other than apologize and move on."

Leena arched one brow. If I didn't know better, I'd say she looked impressed.

"Any more quips? Barbed comments?" I continued.

Leena shook her head with a twisted smile on her mouth.

"Good. Now, show me all of the data you have on this mystery plant."

Leena retrieved three datapads from her desk. "This one has the notes on the soil samples from all of the craters," she explained and handed the first one to me. "The other two have my notes. One is just about the memory-altering chemical, the other has everything else."

It took me a little less than an hour to read through everything. I couldn't help but feel disappointed. I'd expected more.

With a sigh, I set the datapads down.

"Well?" Leena asked expectantly.

"Well, what?" I asked.

"What are we dealing with?"

"How could you expect me to know that?" I replied. "From the information given, I can only tell you what you already know. This is an entirely new species of sentient plant. The genetic analysis was helpful, but it can only tell me what this plant isn't, not what it is."

"Looks like you're going to have to deliver some disappointing news to General Rouhr." Leena folded her arms across her chest.

"Take me to him," I shrugged. "He seemed like a reasonable male when I met him briefly."

Leena led me back through the uniform hallways of the building until we reached General Rouhr's office. Rokul was nowhere to be found. I wondered if General Rouhr had let him off probation.

The flicker of disappointment in my chest when I realized Rokul wasn't around surprised me.

Yes, we agreed to keep things professional, but that didn't change the fact that we'd almost drunkenly screwed in the middle of a dirt road the night before.

I kinda wished we hadn't agreed.

I kinda wished we hadn't stopped.

I wondered how long it would take for my heart to not react when I thought about it.

Leena knocked on the general's door.

The first time I met him, I was too busy taking

everything else in and being shuffled from person to person to get a good look at him.

General Rouhr was a Skotan, like Rokul, though the general's skin wasn't as vibrant. He had a long scar running down the length of his face, but I wouldn't call him disfigured. He had a commanding presence, but there was also kindness in his eyes that I found reassuring.

"What can I do for you, Dr. Dewitt?" he asked Leena.

"Our botanist has news," she said. I wanted to shoot her a glare but not in front of the general. For once in my life, I should at least *try* to maintain a professional air.

"Of course," the general smiled, and offered us a seat in his office.

"I prefer to stand." I smiled so he knew I wasn't being intentionally rude. "And this won't take long."

"I didn't expect to hear back from you so soon," General Rouhr replied. "What can you tell us about the plant creature?"

"That's the thing," I said, suddenly feeling nervous. I didn't know what it was about General Rouhr, but I really didn't want to disappoint him. "Based on the current information, there isn't anything I can tell you about the sentient plant that you don't already know."

"Oh." General Rouhr's brows drew together. "That's

a shame. Leena was so certain you could find something."

"I'm willing to collect new information," I said quickly. "Perhaps, if I could go to this crater and see this creature for myself, I could find something useful."

"At the moment, I'm not authorizing any trips out to the site. I can't afford to lose any team members," General Rouhr replied.

I gave him an apologetic look. "I'm sorry. I want to help," I assured him. "However, there isn't anything I can do with this current information."

"I understand." General Rouhr offered me a kind smile that alleviated a small fraction of my guilt.

"If you decide to allow trips to the crater, please contact me," I said. "Until then, I'll start work at my new position."

"What position?" General Rouhr asked.

"Just before Leena contacted me, I was hired on as a botanist at another lab in Nyheim. The last botanist moved away. I'm taking her place," I explained. "I can leave my information so you can reach me."

"That would be great." General Rouhr passed me a datapad and I entered my information at the new lab.

He looked it over and smiled. "What a surprise. The geologist who initially discovered the creature out in the desert works at that lab, as well. Her name is Annie

Parker. She's recently become engaged to one of my strike team leaders."

"How lovely." I grinned, not knowing what else to say.

"Good luck in your new position," General Rouhr said warmly. "I hope we'll have a reason to contact you soon."

ROKUL

General Rouhr made me fill out an unnecessarily long report covering the events in Rigkon. I left out the part where Tella and I nearly drank ourselves into a stupor and ended up on top of each other in the middle of the outpost's road.

But I thought about it for far longer than I should have.

Reports are not one of my strong points. I'm not fond of sitting at a desk and spending valuable time transcribing the day's events so they can be filed away and never looked at again. Usually, I could convince Takar to write my reports for me. He's much better at them. I'd even go as far as to say that he liked them.

Nearly three hours after Rouhr sent me to write up the report, I knocked on his office door.

"Come in," he called. When he saw it was me, he gave me a smug smile. "Ah, have you finished?"

"Yes, sir." I placed the datapad on his desk.

"Did you learn anything valuable from this little exercise?" General Rouhr asked.

"You and I both know the answer to that question," I shrugged. "But I'll try to think more about consequences. Still think it wouldn't hurt to at least try a few grenades."

General Rouhr sighed and shook his head.

"You're lucky you're a phenomenal soldier," he said. "If you weren't, I'd stick you on one of the ground teams. Dismissed."

"Sir," I paused.

"Was there something else?" General Rouhr asked.

"I just wanted to know how Tella, the botanist, settled in," I said. Even something as simple as saying her name brought everything back. The perfect way she tasted when I kissed her, the feel of her skin.

"Dr. Briar found our current information on the creature in the desert insufficient," General Rouhr explained. "She explained to me that she can't tell us anything new without more data. She's gone to her new position in the same lab where Annie Parker works."

"Oh." I didn't understand why I felt disappointed. True, I looked forward to seeing her around the building, but now that she technically wasn't my colleague anymore, I didn't see a reason to keep things professional. "Will she be back?"

"Potentially," General Rouhr nodded. "She wants to go gather data herself. I'm not willing to risk more lives out in the desert just yet."

"Wise choice," I nodded.

"I'm glad you're behind my decisions." I didn't miss the note of sarcasm in his voice.

"That's all, sir." I nodded and left the room.

As I walked in no particular direction, I thought about going to Tella's new place of employment.

I wondered if she'd agree to dinner. Or perhaps we should simply find another bar and have a repeat of last night in Rigkon. I realized that even though it felt like I'd known Tella for a long time, I didn't truly know her.

It was easy to assume that she'd like to go to a place like the Crooked Swiggen, however, would she choose a place like that if there were more options available?

I'd be the first to admit that I wasn't an expert when it came to Nyheim's dining establishments. Takar and I ate at one of three places, all of them cheap, greasy, and nowhere near as good as Snipe's cooking.

Perhaps I ought to let Tella choose the location.

I'd like to lick anything off her lips at the end of the night. I wanted to run my hands all over her.

I was prepared to go talk to her, revved up with

memories of her silky skin, when my comm unit went off.

"Strike Team Two, report to the launch bay. We're departing immediately," Karzin's voice barked at me.

Tella would have to wait.

I rushed to the launch bay. My brother was already there.

"What's going on?" I asked.

"There's been an attack," he said.

"What town?" I asked.

"Not a town, an outpost set up for refugees," he corrected.

"Skrell," I swore. "So they're essentially defenseless."

"All hands accounted for. Let's move!" Karzin ordered.

Takar and I climbed into our aerial unit as Karzin sent coordinates to our unit's nav system. Within minutes, we were all airborne, zooming towards the coordinates.

We reached the outpost in under ten minutes. As I prepared to land the unit, I got a glimpse of what we'd be fighting.

A group of at least six sorvuc violently tore at the flimsy structures. People darted everywhere, looking for a safe place to hide. I watched a sorvuc lash out at a human male. It struck him hard. He flew back fifteen feet.

We were ordered to land our aerial units far away from the fighting to prevent any accidental damage, but those people needed help now.

I veered off course, ignoring the shouts of my brother.

"Don't be stupid, Rokul," he yelled.

"I'm not!" I shouted back.

I landed the aerial unit right in the middle of the outpost. To my surprise and confusion, the sorvuc didn't immediately attack us. They were intensely focused on destroying the structures of the outpost.

"Move, now!" I ordered Takar. "Don't let them destroy anything else. This is all those refugees have." For once, Takar didn't argue against my impulsiveness. He fired his blaster, hitting a sorvuc square in the back. It roared in outrage, but didn't turn its attention to us.

I hadn't stopped to load up on weapons before reporting to the launch bay. Due to how long the general's report had taken me, all I had on me was what I'd brought to Rigkon, both my standard issue blasters and a small blade that wouldn't do much against the thick skin of a sorvuc.

I recalled the kodanos corpse I'd found in the forest before I rescued Tella.

Looking back on it, I felt certain that Tella had something to do with the dead kodanos. I distinctly remembered the dead kodanos had one shattered leg.

"Shoot for the legs!" I instructed Takar. "If we immobilize them, we can take them down."

"The blasters are hardly effective," he called back. "Shoot the same one as I am." Together, Takar and I fired a few blaster shots into the left leg of the closest sorvuc. Finally, its leg splintered messily. When it took its next step, it lost its balance and fell to the ground. Now, we had their attention.

The rest of my strike team appeared out of the forest. One look at Karzin told me he was furious. I'd deal with that later.

"Shoot at the legs!" I called to Karzin and the others. "Once they're down, leave them. We can pick them off after."

"Do as he says," Karzin backed me up.

Perhaps I wouldn't get placed on probation again after all. The sorvuc abandoned their quest to destroy all of the structures in the outpost. Now their goal was to destroy us. They weren't graceful creatures. Evading them wasn't a challenge.

As I dodged and fired my blaster, I recalled everything I'd learned about sorvuc since arriving on this planet. One thing stuck out as unusual to me. I'd never seen more than one sorvuc at the same time. To see six all at once was surprising.

Perhaps I'd bring it up to Tella before I asked her to dinner. She'd like to know about that, I'd bet.

When the last sorvuc fell, writhing on the ground in outrage, we each took a sorvuc and put it out of its misery. Karzin took down two.

"Locate civilians. Assess injuries. Survey damage," Karzin ordered. I nodded and the strike team fanned out. I went straight to the human male that I'd seen struck by the sorvuc. He was still breathing, half unconscious, and his leg was most certainly broken.

"I've got a serious injury," I called to Karzin.

"I'll call Evie and ask her to dispatch an emergency evac vehicle. Locate others," Karzin ordered. Instead, I knelt down beside the human male.

"Can you understand me?" I asked. His eyelids kept fluttering. He couldn't manage to keep them open or keep them shut. That didn't appear to be a good sign, but I still didn't know much about human bodies. Their immune strength, pain tolerance, and general resilience varied considerably from person to person.

I was certain this human had suffered a blow to the head. I remember Evie saying that humans that have received a blow to the head should not be allowed to fall asleep.

"Open your eyes," I ordered the human male. He tried to keep them open. Every time they started to flutter closed again, I barked another order. It wasn't the best way to deal with the situation, but it was working. From the sound of my voice alone, he was likely too afraid to disobey. If it kept him alive, I'd live with that.

Within an hour, Evie's emergency evacuation transport units arrived. They landed beside my aerial unit. Trained medical professionals poured out of the evac units. I stepped back and allowed them to do their work.

Karzin stood in the center of the activity, watching everything with a critical eye.

"How bad is it?" I asked him.

"You'd have a better idea of that if you'd followed orders," he said reproachfully.

"I didn't think the human I found would survive if he was left alone," I replied.

"For a change, that's an acceptable reason," he nodded. "No deaths, nine major injuries, and thirty minor injuries. Most of the structures serving as temporary homes were damaged. The central structures took less damage."

"Why did they do this?" I wondered out loud.

"They're aggressive sentient trees that have given us trouble on more than one occasion. Are you surprised?" Karzin laughed without humor.

I wanted to tell him that this attack seemed different, but I wasn't sure how to put it into words. Before I could say anything, he spoke again.

"You broke protocol," he said.

"I know."

"I'm going to have to report that to the general," he said.

"I know," I repeated.

"I realize that if you hadn't, more damage would've been done to the outpost and the civilians. I'll include that in my report," Karzin said.

"I'd appreciate that."

Once the emergency medical team loaded all of the injured civilians onto the evac transport units, Karzin addressed the remaining, uninjured civilians.

"You are all welcome to go to Nyheim for temporary shelter while this outpost is being rebuilt," he told them. Most of them were still in shock and didn't react. A handful of emergency medical responders stayed behind to assist them to the city.

As I climbed back into my aerial unit, Takar spoke up.

"You're in deep skrell, you know that?"

"I'm aware."

I was equally aware I probably wasn't going on any dates any time soon.

TELLA

I'd been here for less than a day and I was already feeling twitchy and restless. Apparently, Bea, the botanist before me, wasn't a popular woman. To put it simply, she annoyed the crap out of everyone on her floor. Everyone on Bea's old floor was so concerned that I would be annoying that I was assigned to a different lab station on a different floor.

Whoever Bea was, she'd manage to convince everyone in the building that all botanists were chatty, nosy, and pushy.

Thanks, Bea.

My new lab station was in the farthest corner of the room, facing a wall. If I wanted to look out a window, I'd have to crane my neck at an uncomfortable angle. Not that the view was great in the first place. The single wall sporting windows faced the side of another beat-up building in the middle of being repaired.

The ceiling lights were too yellow, as if they were trying to mimic sunlight and failed horribly. The building did have a cooling system, but in my little corner, I couldn't feel it. I felt like I'd been stuffed in a box and I hated it. There wasn't even a balcony I could step onto to get a quick breath of fresh air.

I tried telling myself that I simply needed to get used to my new surroundings, but I knew myself. This kind of environment was not one where I thrived. My element was out in the field studying live specimens first hand.

As I took some time to acquaint myself with the console system, my mind wandered to Rokul.

I preferred solitude when I worked, but it was never a smart idea to go out into the field alone. I hadn't anticipated Gille's job to be as dangerous as it was, so I hadn't hired a mercenary to accompany me. I hated working with mercenaries. They were impatient, had no respect for the environment around them, and tended to be full of themselves.

Rokul possessed all of those traits, yet I didn't despise him. In fact, if I were to take another field assignment, I would ask him to join me before I went to a mercenary. I thought about how he'd killed the Helmria Ithalma. Yes, I was pissed about it since the flower was so rare, but if he hadn't killed it, it certainly would've killed us.

I felt guilty for leaving General Rouhr's building without saying goodbye to Rokul, but I didn't know where he was or how to find him. If I did manage to find him, I wouldn't have known what to say.

It was fun getting drunk with you, I'll see you later?

Sorry you had to retrieve me as part of your punishment, let's hang out sometime?

Yeah, those both sounded incredibly stupid in my head and would've sounded even stupider out loud. Maybe it was for the best that I hadn't seen him before I left.

"Are you the new botanist?" A woman's voice startled me out of my thoughts. A petite woman around my age with pin-straight red hair smiled at me.

"Yes," I nodded. "My name's Tella Briar." I extended a hand and she shook it.

"Annie Parker," she replied. "I'm a geologist." I recognized her name.

"You're the one who took those soil samples, aren't you?" I asked. "The ones for the weird plant out in the desert."

"That's right." She looked surprised that I would know that for a moment before realization took over her expression. "Are you Leena Dewitt's friend? She mentioned she was reaching out to a botanist contact of hers."

"Yes, that's me," I replied.

"So, you've seen all the data on that thing in the desert," she prompted.

"I have." I didn't want to tell her that I found her data insufficient for my work. That wasn't a good way to make friends.

"Why aren't you working in General Rouhr's building?" she asked, tilting her head to one side. "I would think he'd want you working around the clock to figure out what that plant is."

"I was there earlier," I replied. It seemed that there was no getting around it. "Leena showed me all the information on the creature. Unfortunately, it didn't tell me very much. The best I could do was confirm what everyone already knows about it."

"I see," Annie frowned. She didn't look angry, just disappointed. "When I compiled the information, I knew it wouldn't be very helpful. Since it's a new species, I knew you'd need to collect your own data to help General Rouhr."

"Exactly." I breathed a sigh of relief. "I really want to help, so I gave Rouhr my information here so he could contact me if he decides to let me go out to the crater myself. Until then, I'm going to start my work here."

"I'm glad to have you," Annie grinned. "The last botanist was-"

"Annoying?" I said before she could finish her thought.

"Thanks for not making me say it out loud," she chuckled. "Bea was an interesting character, to say the least."

"So I've heard," I grimaced. "She's left me notes to continue her last project. I haven't read them yet, but there are nearly twenty pages of material."

"That sounds like Bea," Annie replied. "She's probably included a few personal anecdotes in those notes."

"I hope she's an entertaining writer," I laughed. "I'll be reading these for a while."

"I'm at the station near the windows if you need anything," Annie offered kindly.

"I'm jealous," I replied. "How does one get a station by a window?"

"I was at the one you're at now until I started working with General Rouhr," Annie replied.

"I hope General Rouhr calls me in soon so I can get a better station," I joked.

Annie smiled before returning to her own work. I picked up the datapad left for me by Bea. After fifteen minutes of reading, I came to the conclusion that her notes were ninety percent tangents and personal stories.

From what I gathered, Bea was about to start monitoring the current populations of sentient plant species. The odd part was she wasn't planning any field expeditions to gather her own data. Bea planned to compile data from other botanists' field research. I laughed out loud when I saw that one of my previous studies was on her list.

With nothing else to do, I turned to my console and picked up where she'd left off. Bea had gathered a list of studies, but hadn't actually compiled anything. Additionally, she was short about eight studies if she wanted to get an accurate reflection of the current sentient plant population.

My study was included in the list of studies that had measured the population before the Xathi invasion. It was the studies done after the Xathi invasion that were seriously lacking. The other botanists on this world were probably in the same shape I was. Expeditions were going to be difficult to get underway.

However, now that I had this lab at my disposal, perhaps the manager would agree to allocate some funds to further my study. I could ask Rokul to join me. The idea brought a smile to my face.

The lab was run by a woman called Dr. Madriana

Hines. Aside from introducing myself to her earlier today, I had yet to have a conversation with the woman.

I didn't feel nervous as I left the main lab and walked down to Dr. Hines's office. I was prepared to knock on the door, but her door was wide open.

"Hello, Tella," she smiled warmly. "Are you settling in?"

"Yes. I actually came to talk to you about the procedure for requesting funds," I said. Dr. Hines looked confused. "For fieldwork," I added.

"Oh!" Her brows shot up in surprise. "I don't mean to cause offense, but I usually reserve those funds for employees who've shown me that they can provide results. I don't know you yet."

"You know I have the experience," I tried to convince her without being pushy. "I don't think you would've hired me otherwise."

"I understand where you're coming from," she said. "However, I cannot authorize a field expedition on your first day. It wouldn't look good to the other scientists with pending expedition applications."

Ah, so it was a game of politics.

Give me lethal walking trees any day.

"Thank you for your time," I said with a smile I hoped didn't look too forced. As I made my way back to my lab station, I contemplated leaving this job. I could get by on little gigs like the one offered by Gilles. I didn't have to lock myself away in a lab.

When I returned to the main lab room, I saw that my comm unit was beeping.

That was odd. Very few people knew how to contact my comm unit.

"Hello?" I asked.

"Dr. Tella Briar?" My chest tightened as I recognized General Rouhr's voice.

"Yes. Sir. General." Oh hell. "Is everything well?" I asked, floundering.

"I have news you may find interesting. I know you were just here, but would you mind returning to my office?"

I covered the comm unit so he wouldn't hear me squeal with excitement.

"Are you there?" he asked. I quickly removed my hand.

"Yes! Yes, I'll come right over. Thank you!" I exclaimed. General Rouhr laughed.

"I'm glad to know you're so enthusiastic," he chuckled. "I'll see you soon. Security will be made aware that you're coming in. You shouldn't have any trouble accessing the building."

"Thanks again!" I said before the line disconnected.

"Sounds like good news," Annie called from across the lab.

"General Rouhr called me back in," I replied with a grin so huge it hurt my cheeks. I gathered my things, checked in with Dr. Hines, and left the dismal lab. I was overflowing with excitement, but not just for the potential work to come.

New information meant clues, meant getting out of this confining box.

And maybe out into the field.

And just maybe, possibly, seeing a certain Skotan again.

All those things were pretty exciting. But I was pretty sure only one had sparked the butterflies in my stomach.

ROKUL

As soon as General Rouhr disconnected from Tella's comm unit, his face changed from pleasant to cold fury.

And as usual lately, that anger was directed at one target.

Me.

The moment he called me into his office, I made a point of telling him about the strange behavior of the sorvuc.

Naturally, his first thought was to call Tella. I'd be lying if I said that wasn't exactly what I wanted to happen. I was all too aware of what would happen after he called Tella in, but knowing she was on her way would make what was coming sting a little less.

"I don't think I have to tell you that you went

against protocol," General Rouhr said in a low voice. "What I cannot comprehend is that you, knowing full well how devastating recent attacks have been, and knowing that we're dealing with an unpredictable enemy we know nothing about, can make the decision to ignore the orders of your team leader and your superior."

"I did not break from protocol until I knew that we were dealing with something other than that creature out in the desert," I argued.

"What does that matter?" General Rouhr snapped.

"That protocol was put in place to dictate our plan of attack in the event that a human settlement was specifically attacked by the creature. It was not the creature that attacked, therefore the protocol no longer applied," I reasoned.

I knew my argument fell into what humans referred to as a gray area. Technically, I was right. But only technically.

"I should demote you to a ground team," General Rouhr growled. "They're working night and day building homes for displaced humans. They're being useful and making a difference, which is more than I can say for you."

"The sorvuc were stopped and no humans died," I replied in the least-argumentative tone I could manage, even though I wanted to shout. I heard Takar's voice in my mind telling me that being aggressive and argumentative would get me nowhere.

"You wouldn't be here talking to me if a human had died," General Rouhr snapped. "You would've been shipped off to the farthest ground team camp before you returned to this building."

I appreciate what the ground teams were doing for the humans. General Rouhr was right when he said they made a difference. They gave terrified families roofs to sleep under and food to eat, then guarded said families while they enjoyed their food and sleep. I had nothing but respect for the ground teams and I felt eager to help the humans.

However, the best way I could do that was being part of my strike team. General Rouhr could stick me on a ground team and I would do just fine, but Takar and I had spent five years training for our positions. It would be difficult to put a ground team member in my place and expect the same results.

Difficult, but maybe not impossible.

If a human had died or if we hadn't stopped the sorvuc, I would've understood General Rouhr's anger better.

"I know our operations only work if communication is adequate, but-"

"Not adequate!" General Rouhr threw his datapad down on his desk hard enough that I was surprised that it didn't crack. "Exemplary. If you do not communicate with your team, your team will fail."

"Of course, sir," I nodded. "But if I didn't land when I did, I wouldn't have been able to figure out the best plan of attack for my team when they arrived on the scene. The moment they arrived they knew to shoot at the legs of the sorvuc to immobilize them."

I wasn't going to back down. I hadn't followed protocol, but I'd done the right thing. If I was sent away to work on a ground team, I wouldn't be able to take care of real threats and stop those threats from killing more people.

The thing out in the desert could reach cities and human settlements. It was a real threat. I needed to be here fighting against it. I needed to be here fighting against raging herds of sorvuc, too, for that matter.

"I got here as soon as I could!" Tella burst into General Rouhr's office. Her cheeks were pink, flushed from exertion. She was out of breath like she'd been running. My eyes were drawn to the rise and fall of her chest and, despite the situation, the sight was magnificent, the swell of her chest matching a sudden swell in my trousers. Visions of her underneath me, with that same flushed exertion, threatened to remove my entire ability to focus.

I tightened my fist, then unclenched it as I pulled my eyes away from the perfect curve of her breasts, the delicious color of her skin. Memories of her taste, the feel of her, flooded through my consciousness and I ached to do nothing but pull her into my arms now.

"I called you at your lab station's comm unit," General Rouhr said slowly, looking as surprised as I felt. "You ran here that quickly?"

"It was no trouble. I've spent most of my career outrunning things that were trying to kill me." Tella's chuckle came out more like a wheeze. I laughed under my breath. Tella's eyes flickered in my direction. Her expression shifted when she realized I was in the room.

She straightened up and made an attempt to brush away the errant hairs that had escaped from her braid, though it didn't make a difference. I think the fastening that held her braid in place had fallen out of her hair when she ran here. The braid itself still held its shape, though one more good shake of her head would loosen it completely. I had a sudden urge to run my fingers through her dark locks. I swallowed hard and forced the urge away.

Now wasn't the time.

There might never be a time.

"Please, have a seat." General Rouhr gestured to the chair I currently sat in. I knew he meant to knock me down a notch or two by forcing me to give up my seat. He blinked once in surprise when I eagerly leaped out of the chair and offered it to Tella.

"Thanks," she said to both General Rouhr and me.

"Glad you're back," I said quickly, my eyes watching her lips as she smiled at me.

"You will wait outside while I talk to Dr. Briar," General Rouhr ordered.

"Yes, sir," I nodded. Before I left the office, I reached out and gave Tella's shoulder a quick squeeze.

I closed the door to give General Rouhr the privacy he so clearly desired, but I didn't leave. Inside, Tella and the general began to talk but I couldn't make out any distinct words.

General Rouhr should've let me give Tella the details about the sorvuc. I was there, after all. I wanted to see Tella's expression when I described their behavior. I also wanted to hear her thoughts. I knew I'd hear the main points from her later or, more likely, General Rouhr. It irked me that I wasn't there to hear her opinion on the matter, first hand.

"No matter how hard you scowl at the paint, it's not going to answer you." My brother leaned against the wall next to me.

"How come you're never in trouble with me, yet you're always there when I'm getting into trouble?" I grumbled.

"Because I have no desire to be part of trouble. You're just exceptionally talented at dragging me into it," Takar replied. "Was that the botanist I saw sprinting through the building like a creature gone mad?"

"Yes," I smiled.

"What's so important that she couldn't simply walk?" Takar asked.

"She was over at the same lab where Annie works. I haven't seen the place myself, but Karzin tells me it's nothing like the lab we have here or the lab on the *Aurora*," I replied.

"Nothing compares to the *Aurora*," Takar said fondly, "but what does that have to do with the botanist?"

"Tella isn't fond of working indoors," I explained. "Even the *Aurora* would take second place if she had the option to work in the field."

"Tella?" Takar looked at me with a raised brow.

"That's her name. It's not unusual that I should use it. I spent several hours with her in Rigkon," I said defensively. I hated it when Takar gave me that look.

"I still don't fully understand why you were required to spend the night there." Takar gave me a knowing look.

"I told you. Tella needed to collect payment for the completion of the job she was hired to do." I must've told him that three times already.

"I thought you would've wanted to get back here and off probation as soon as possible," Takar said.

"Of course," I shrugged. "But would it have been right of me to deny a hardworking woman her honest wages?"

"I suppose not." Takar dropped the matter, but I didn't like the note of suspicion in his voice.

"We're just friends," I said firmly. "Not even that. We had a few drinks, talked, and didn't hate each other. End of story."

"If you say so."

I didn't believe me either. My words were punctuated with the searing memories of Tella's body pressed against mine, her lips parting for mine. Claiming her, capturing her, having her in a moment where time stood still.

Not that I'd say that aloud to my brother.

General Rouhr's door opened and Takar and I immediately stood to attention.

"Don't you have work to do, Takar?" the general asked.

"Yes, sir." Takar nodded and walked down the corridor.

"Rokul, your presence has been requested." General Rouhr's voice carried as much surprise as I felt. I stepped into the office. Tella sat in the chair, smiling as I walked in.

"Doctor Briar doesn't find the information about the sorvuc to be sufficient. She can't make any conclusions concerning whether or not their behavior was odd based on the incident reports," General Rouhr explained.

I turned to Tella.

"I can give you a firsthand account of the sorvuc's behavior if you'd find that useful," I offered. General Rouhr looked at me with the same suspicion in his expression that I heard in Takar's voice.

Was it really so hard for others to believe I could be nice?

"Dr. Briar has already decided that she needs to examine the sorvuc bodies herself," General Rouhr answered for her. "And, for some reason, she refuses to go unless you guard her."

I looked at Tella from the corner of my eye. She looked pleased with herself.

"If that's what our botanist needs, I'll happily oblige," I grinned.

"Good. Leave tomorrow. Both of you have been doing enough running around today," General Rouhr ordered. "Dismissed."

TELLA

By the time General Rouhr arranged everything so that I could go to the location of the sorvuc attack, it was well after sundown. I spent the night in a rented room above a tavern called the Blooming Bud, which I found pleasantly ironic.

If I'd never set foot inside the Crooked Swiggen, I would've called the Blooming Bud run down. My sister Gracie would've called it charmingly rustic.

Shame she'd never get to see it.

Thinking of my sister ensured that I needed to order at least one drink. I stopped at two. I couldn't show up hungover to my first official day of work for General Rouhr.

When I woke up the next morning, I felt as close to refreshed as someone like me could. Nowadays, the only way for me to get a good night's sleep was to drink myself into a stupor. Sleep wasn't worth the damage drinking did to my body, so I made a rule to only drink when I thought of my family.

Or if I was stuck in a crappy half-town with a handsome alien companion.

Speaking of handsome alien companions, Rokul was already waiting for me in the main lobby when I walked into General Rouhr's building.

"I expected you to be late," Rokul grinned.

"Why would you think that?" I asked.

"If I hadn't woken you up the other morning, you would've slept all day," he reasoned.

"Maybe so," I admitted. "However, when I'm not stumbling over myself, I'm a pretty light sleeper."

"Let me guess. It's because you've spent many nights sleeping in the forest vulnerable to all sorts of nasty creatures," Rokul said.

"That's right," I laughed. "It seems that I'm becoming predictable."

"Never," Rokul grinned. "The general's assigned us an aerial unit for the day. I'm ready to go when you are."

I double checked to make sure I had everything I needed in my supply pack. Years ago, I'd developed the habit of keeping a pack ready to go so I didn't have to scramble in the morning to get everything ready.

When I was satisfied, I nodded to Rokul.

We walked through the building to the launch bay. I noticed that Rokul and I received a lot of odd looks as we walked.

"Why are the others staring at us?" I leaned closer to him and whispered.

"They don't believe we could've spent a night together, but in separate beds, after a night of heavy drinking," he whispered back.

"How do they know about that?" I asked.

"There's no such thing as a secret in a tight-knit group like this. My strike team knew I spent the night in Rigkon, my brother knew I'd been drinking the moment he saw me, and the moment everyone here laid eyes on you, they began to piece things together," Rokul explained.

"I'm not sure if I should be flattered or not," I said dryly.

"Oh, you should," Rokul assured me. "I've been doing my best to stamp out any rumors, but my denial only seems to make me appear guiltier."

"That sounds about right," I nodded. "Did you tell me you had a brother?"

"I don't believe I did," Rokul replied. "You'll likely meet him eventually. He's nothing like me, so if you find me insufferable, you'll get along with him."

"I don't find you insufferable."

I should've found him insufferable. On paper, he

was the exact sort of person I used to avoid. How we were able to get on so well was beyond me, but I certainly wasn't going to question it too much. It was high time that I made some friends, or whatever it was that Rokul was becoming.

"Is that why you told General Rouhr that you wouldn't go look at the sorvuc remains without me?" He flashed an arrogant grin that I would've found insufferable if he weren't so damn charismatic.

"I refused to go without you because I already know I can rely on you should things go awry," I explained. It was the truth, but not the whole truth. I also wanted to spend time with him but I didn't want to inflate his ego by admitting that. "I know I won't have to carry you."

"I'd happily carry you if you needed me to," he joked. "But I know you can handle yourself." His words sparked an odd, warm feeling inside me.

The aerial unit General Rouhr allocated for us to use seemed pretty beat up compared to the others. Its engine made a loud rattling noise that made me uneasy.

Rokul just laughed. "It's noisy, but beats freezing in a rift!" he shouted. "Fen can keep working on that as long as she wants, as far as I care."

That… didn't make any sense. Or make me feel better.

On the way over to the outpost the sorvuc had attacked, we attempted to make conversation, but the rattle of the engine drowned out half our words. We ended up sitting in comfortable not-quite-silence, tapping each other and pointing when we saw something interesting through the unit's windows.

When we landed, I started to let Rokul help me out of the unit, though I could've climbed out myself. When his hand touched the bare skin of my forearm, my heart did a weird jump. He surprised me by slipping his arm under the crook of my knees and wrapping his other arm around my back. He picked me up as if I weighed nothing and carried me a few paces before setting me down.

"I told you I could carry you," he grinned.

"I never doubted that," I laughed, hoping the pink on my cheeks wouldn't mean anything to him. "Show me the bodies."

My biggest worry was that something might've happened to the dead sorvuc overnight that would prevent me from obtaining accurate data today, but when I saw the first sorvuc corpse, nothing looked amiss.

"How many were there in total?" I asked.

"Six. They should all be here," he replied.

"That's highly unusual. Sorvuc are solitary creatures. They don't even come together to mate. They mate like ordinary plants," I explained.

"That's what I thought," Rokul replied.

"Did your team do that to their legs?" I asked.

"Yes." Roku looked proud. "I saw a kodanos with the same leg injury the day I went looking for you. It looked like a smart idea."

"I did that," I grinned.

"Not surprising," Rokul replied. There it was again, that little happy flutter in my stomach that made me feel valued. And maybe something else.

"Sorvuc are fairly aggressive," I said as I continued my examination. "I take it they were behaving aggressively here."

"Yes, but they were moving quicker than I've ever seen one move and targeting the structures, not the humans," Rokul explained.

I frowned and drummed my finger on my leg. Sorvuc usually avoided manmade structures. They knew there wasn't anything for them there. When Rokul said they moved quicker than normal, the memory of the speeding kodanos came to mind.

"I want to check something," I murmured more to myself than to Rokul. I unsheathed my hunting knife and drove it into the sorvuc's back. I sliced through its armor-like bark until I could pry its body open. Inside, I found a tangle of vines similar to those I'd found inside the kodanos.

"See these here?" I pointed to the vines to show Rokul. He nodded. "Those aren't part of the sorvuc."

"Then what are they part of?" he asked.

"I'm not sure." I took out my clippers and snipped off a few fragments from several of the vines. I sealed them in airtight bags and tucked them into my supply pack. "I think it's some kind of invasive species that are using the bodies of sentient plants as a host. Perhaps to spread its own seed."

I moved on to the other sorvuc bodies. Sure enough, every time I cracked one open, I found a nest of vines. I took clippings from each body. I was certain all the vines were from the same species, but I wanted to confirm it in a lab.

I returned to the first corpse to continue my observations. It was in better shape than the other sorvuc, by far.

As I leaned in to get a better look at the intrusive vines, I heard a rustling sound. I looked over my shoulder, expecting to see one of the forest's sentient vines worming its way towards us, but there was nothing there. Yet the rustling continued. It didn't occur to me to look at the sorvuc until something cold and strong wrapped around my forearm.

The vines inside the sorvuc were still alive. I yelped and tried to yank my arm back, but the vine tightened its grip. The vine was wrapped around the arm that held my knife. I rotated my wrist, hoping to slice the vine, but it didn't work.

Rokul was at my side in a heartbeat. I dropped my knife for him to grab. He took it and slashed through the vine right as my arm started to feel numb.

Once I was free, Rokul lifted me up by my arms and pulled me back in the direction of the aerial unit. I didn't take my eyes off the dead sorvuc. The vines inside were writhing and twisting around each other.

Another vine lashed out, this time at the nearest tree. When it found purchase, it started to drag the sorvuc body towards the deeper jungle.

"What the skrell," Rokul exclaimed under his breath. The other sorvuc corpses began moving, too. Vines burst through their tough exteriors and latched on to nearby trees.

Rokul and I watched in stunned silence as the vines dragged the sorvuc bodies beyond the tree line and out of sight. We could still hear the rustling and crunching as they moved away.

"We have to follow them!" I insisted. I started walking, but Rokul still had a grip on my arm.

"Are you insane?" he asked.

"What? Are you scared?" I taunted.

"Of course not," he huffed. "But even I don't think it's wise to charge in blind after those vines. We'd never see them coming in that thick part of the jungle."

"Fine," I grumbled, even though he was right.

"What kind of guard would I be if I let you charge into danger?" he said with a half-smile.

"A crappy one," I nodded.

"Exactly. And until we have a better idea of what's going on, I don't like the idea of us out there." He placed his hand on my lower back to guide me to the aerial unit. I found that I didn't mind the weight.

ROKUL

It was hard to keep my eyes looking straight ahead
with Tella in the seat next to me. Seeing that vine
wrap around her, hearing the little scream that had torn
from her lips, had sent me into overdrive.

I wanted to chop the vines up into little pieces so
they wouldn't touch her again. I refrained only because
I knew Tella would've been angry at me if I had.

At the moment, she had her knees tucked up against
her chest and was using them to support her arms as
she examined one of the vine fragments she'd collected.
She furrowed her brow slightly and ran her fingers
over every inch of the vine fragment.

I found it amazing that she could dedicate her whole
focus to something that most people would've found
mundane and unimportant. I wasn't sure what she was

seeing in that two-inch segment of vine, but it was fascinating to her. She tilted her head and her dark hair slipped off the curve of her shoulder, blocking most of her face from my view.

Without thinking, I took one hand off the pilot console and pushed her hair back over her shoulder. She lifted her head and gave me an odd look. I suddenly felt very foolish, but I wasn't about to let her know that.

I plastered an easy smile on my face.

"What was that for?" she shouted over the rattling of the engine.

"It's fun to watch your face when you're studying chunks of vicious plant matter," I shouted back. To my surprise and relief, her expression relaxed and she smiled.

"It's fun examining vicious plant matter while being chauffeured around by a Skotan warrior," she replied.

"Is that all you think I'm good for?" I made a show of looking offended, which made her laugh.

"Of course not!" she exclaimed. "You're also good for hacking through various things."

"I'm flattered." I rolled my eyes. "Do you have any theories about the vines?"

"There are a few known species of invasive plants, but none that can freely manipulate the body of their host organism," she said, though I only caught about half of her words. The rest were swallowed by the noise of the aerial unit. I understood the essence of what she said, though. "The thing is, these vines don't look like any of those species. I'll have to test them at the lab to know for sure, though."

"What if they're from a previously unknown species?" I asked.

"Then I'll have to find more," she replied. "Hopefully, General Rouhr is more willing to lend me funds for field missions than Dr. Hines is."

"Who?"

"She's my boss at the other lab," I explained. "Despite my damn-near-perfect resume, she doesn't want me to launch any field expeditions because it might hurt the feelings of other scientists in the lab."

"That doesn't make sense," I frowned. "If you're qualified, you should be allowed to do your job."

"Exactly!" She threw her free hand up in frustration. She went back to examining the vine fragments. This time, she compared two of them side by side. I tried to focus on piloting the aerial unit, but I kept sneaking glances at her.

I suddenly felt aware of how little I truly knew about her. Tella was a brilliant botanist, impressive survivalist, and could hold her drink better than half the *Vengeance* crew, but other than that, I didn't know anything else.

There had to be more to her.

I wasn't one to overshare personal details of my life, but even I had sprinkled in personal details about myself in normal conversation. Tella didn't do that, or if she did, she kept her personal details confined to a few specific topics.

I knew she hated being stuck inside and preferred fieldwork over lab work, but I didn't know where she was from, if she had any family on this world, or even simple things like her favorite food.

Obviously, she was a guarded person, but I didn't understand why.

I searched my brain for an excuse to ask her personal questions without violating our agreement to remain professional while we worked together.

What a skrelling stupid thing to have agreed to.

We were clearly attracted to each other. What was the worst that could happen if we decided to form a nonprofessional relationship?

"Do you ever think about the other night in Rigkon?" I blurted over the rattling engine.

"All the time," Tella replied with more candor than I'd expected. When she saw my expression, she spoke again. "Why? Don't you?"

"I think about it constantly. It keeps me up at night," I grinned. From the corner of my eye, I saw her smile.

"It's a shame we work together now," she drawled.

"It really is. I wouldn't mind having a repeat of that

night." I tore my eyes away from the windshield to wink at Tella. She rolled her eyes, but I could see the faintest tinge of blush appear on her cheeks.

"I wouldn't either," she said. "Maybe less of whatever the hell we drank at the Crooked Swiggen, though."

"Agreed. I'd like to remember every second of a night with you." Another peek at her revealed that her blush had deepened. I found it charming that she spoke with the bravado any one of the *Vengeance* crew would use if they were talking about females they'd bedded, yet she blushed like she'd never been touched by a male. The mystery that was Tella deepened.

"It's a shame we agreed to keep things professional," she hummed so softly I almost didn't hear her.

"You're the one who came up with the idea!" I replied. "I just agreed to it because I didn't want you to use that hunting knife on me."

"I wouldn't have used the knife on you," she said, though she didn't sound completely sure about that.

"If you say so," I joked.

"I don't know what I was thinking when I proposed that idea," she mused. "I must've still been drunk."

I knew she wasn't. She knew she wasn't.

"Well, you know what they say about things said when drunk?" I asked.

"What?" She tilted her head to look at me.

"That they are best forgotten when sober," I

finished. Tella chucked and twirled a lock of hair between her fingers. I couldn't tell if it was a flirtatious gesture or a nervous habit.

I could tell that Tella liked people to believe that she was an independent, invincible woman. And she *was* pretty impressive, even to a pretty hard-to-surprise Skotan.

But I wondered if she limited herself to situations where she actually was independent and invincible, with no risk of vulnerability.

My desire to take her out of those situations grew by the minute. I wanted to know the real Tella.

"I think you may be right." She looked over and flashed a smile, though I saw the faintest hint of hesitation in her eyes.

"That's not why I wanted to come with you to see the sorvuc bodies," I added quickly. "I don't want you to think that."

"Don't worry, I don't," she assured me. "Though, why did you want to come along? I know I trapped you by telling General Rouhr I wouldn't go with anyone else. Would you have come along if I hadn't done that?"

"Assuming I knew you were going to look at the sorvuc corpses at the time, I would've asked General Rouhr to let me go with you," I admitted. "That night in Rigkon aside, you're a fantastic partner to have in the field."

Her brows shot up and an unconstrained smile bloomed across her mouth. I realized that, until that moment, I'd never seen a genuine smile from Tella. A genuine *sober* smile, at least. None of her smiles were forced, but she subdued them for some reason.

"Do you really think so?" she asked. It struck me as odd that Tella would need reassurance of any kind. I was learning more secret little things about her in this transport unit than I had in the last few days. I wondered if she knew she was giving me tiny bits of information about her.

"Absolutely!" I exclaimed. "I think you're...hang on, you humans have a perfect word for this. Let me think. Badass! I think you're a badass." Tella tipped her head back and laughed.

"I think you're a badass, too," she said when she caught her breath.

"Then it's only fair to us, as two attractive badasses, to not limit our relationship to anything," I proposed. She gave me a playfully suspicious smile.

"How long have you planned that line?" she asked.

"I came up with it in the moment," I answered. "Though I've been thinking about it since the morning we woke up in that guesthouse."

"Me, too," she admitted. "So, where do we go from here?"

"Wherever we want," I grinned.

"Sounds nice," she smiled. "But first, let's figure out this plant problem." She lifted up one of the bags containing a vine sample and gave it a little shake.

"I'm at your command." I was only half joking.

At that point, I felt like I would do anything Tella asked me to.

We fell into contented silence as we neared Nyheim. Out of the corner of my eye, I saw her place her hand on the low seat divider between us. I placed my hand on top of hers and traced patterns on her skin with the tips of my fingers.

She laced her fingers with mine. As we arrived back at the capital city, our hands lazily fought for dominance over the other. Her skin was soft and smooth, and I was burning with slow, steady desire to know what the rest of her felt like.

TELLA

I jumped out of the aerial unit before it was fully docked.

"Hey!" Rokul shouted after me as he finally shut off the rattling engine.

"I want to get these to the lab right away!" I shouted back.

"I'll handle the report to General Rouhr, then," he offered.

"Thanks! I'll see you in a bit!" I was already halfway out of the launch bay when I spoke. I truly was excited to test the vine samples in General Rouhr's lab. His equipment was better than what Dr. Hines had in her lab.

However, I also wanted to spend some time away

from Rokul to seriously think about what we'd talked about on the ride back.

As I made my way to the lab, I replayed our conversation over and over in my head. The more I thought about it, the less sure I was about what I was signing myself up for. Yes, we both wanted to stop pretending we only wanted a professional relationship, but were we on the same page?

I wasn't sure what page *I* was on, let alone what page *he* was on.

I didn't think he was talking about being friends outside of work. Our miniature finger war confirmed that for me.

But did Rokul want to be in a relationship, or was he just looking for some fun on the side? What was I looking for, for that matter?

Drinking with him at the Crooked Swiggen was the most fun I'd had in years that didn't involve a sentient plant attempting to kill me.

The thing was, I really liked him. I hadn't known him long, and I really didn't know much about him, but I still had a feeling that we could be really good together. But if he was just looking for fun, I didn't want to open myself up to him like that.

Even if he wasn't just looking for fun, did I still want to open myself up to a male? A Skotan male, no less.

Not that I had any problem with the fact that he wasn't a human. I liked the way his vibrantly red skin looked. I thought it was fascinating to watch his scales expand and retract when he fought. And I didn't think we'd ever run out of things to talk about when I knew so little about his species.

After losing my parents and my sister during the Xathi invasion, I hadn't let myself get close to another person.

I'd already lost so much, I couldn't bear the idea of losing anyone else. If I allowed myself to get close to Rokul, I had to be ready to accept the fact that there was a chance I'd lose him in the end.

Besides, even if I was ready to get close to someone like that, I didn't know if I was still capable of doing so. I'd gotten used to doing everything alone. It was easy to protect myself when I was alone.

With thoughts of Rokul, family, and loneliness still spinning in my head, I entered the lab. Leena was there talking to a tall, dark-haired woman.

"Tella." Leena sounded surprised. "I didn't realize you were coming in. My sister, Mariella, stopped by to say hello." I'd never met Mariella, but I'd heard Leena say some unkind things about her when we worked at the university. It looked like they'd mended the rift between them.

"Hi," I nodded to Mariella before turning to Leena. "General Rouhr called me in yesterday. He wanted me to look into some sorvuc that were acting strangely. I have some samples to test."

"We won't bother you, will we?" Mariella asked with a genuine smile that made me want to smile, too.

"Not at all," I assured her. As I prepped my vine samples for testing, Mariella and Leena picked up their conversation once more. I tried not to listen, but since they were the only noise in the room, it was impossible not to.

"I just came from Jeneva's home," Mariella said. I'd heard the name Jeneva in passing a few times, but I'd never met her.

"How is she?" Leena asked with a level of concern I wouldn't have thought she possessed.

"She's very tired all the time," Mariella sighed. "The baby is really giving her a hard time. Doctors come to her house twice a day."

"If it's giving her a hard time now, imagine what it'll be like when it's born," Leena said. "Do they know the gender?"

"Not yet. I think Jeneva wants it to be a surprise," Mariella explained.

I sliced off an impossibly small piece of each vine and prepared them for microscopic viewing. Then I cut larger slices and prepared them for genetic testing.

"Vrehx must be worried sick," Leena said. "I haven't seen him in weeks."

"General Rouhr's put him on leave until the baby is born. I saw him while I was at Jeneva's. I've never seen a Skotan look so pale."

I froze midway through preparing the genetic testing machine. Did Mariella just say Skotan? I put the pieces together in my mind. Jeneva was a human woman having a child with a Skotan male. That didn't sound possible. No wonder the pregnancy was rough.

"Do you think you and Tu'ver will have kids soon?" Leena asked her sister.

"We aren't even married yet!" Mariella laughed. "I always assumed we'd have kids. But if carrying a K'ver child is anything like carrying a Skotan child, I'll have to prepare myself in advance." Mariella was with a K'ver?

"Axtin and I both thought we never wanted kids, but we're both coming around to the idea," Leena said sheepishly.

"A Valorni baby is going to be huge!" Mariella exclaimed with a laugh. "You'd look so funny carrying such a big baby."

Were all of the human women I occasionally saw around the building paired with an alien male? Was that becoming a common thing now? I considered bringing up Rokul and joining the conversation, but what would I say?

I may or may not be considering casually sleeping with a Skotan I might actually have true feelings for?

Not exactly in the same line, not when they were talking about marriage and babies.

I kept my mouth shut and focused on my work. While the genetic test ran, I looked at the smaller samples through the microscope. The cell structure of the vines was similar to other sentient vine species I'd studied. In fact, the cell structure of the vines looked almost identical to the cell structure of parent plants the current species had evolved from. The vines controlling the sorvuc corpses were old.

Ancient, even.

"You really need to pick a date for the wedding," Leena said. I'd somehow tuned back in to their conversation.

"It just feels wrong to have a wedding while the planet is still rebuilding," Mariella replied. "It would feel like I'm flaunting my happiness and good fortune in front of thousands who lost everything."

"You don't want to get married because you don't want to hurt strangers' feelings?" Leena said slowly.

"Exactly," Mariella said with confidence.

The genetic analysis machine beeped, startling me from my eavesdropping. That was one thing I absolutely loved about the lab machines in General Rouhr's building. They were all so fast and amazingly accurate. I wondered which species brought in this tech. My guess was the K'ver.

I sent the genetic analysis from the machine to my datapad. When I pulled up the data, I noticed that it looked familiar.

"Hey, Leena?" I called.

"Yeah?" she replied.

"Do you have the analysis on the genetic material from the crater?" I asked.

"Right here." She picked a datapad up off her desk and handed it to me. "Why?"

"Look at this." I placed both sets of data next to each other. They were identical.

"The thing in the crater is a sorvuc?" Leena asked, brow furrowed.

"The samples I took weren't from the sorvuc," I explained. "They came from parasitic vines still living inside the sorvuc corpses."

"I don't understand." Mariella walked over and stood beside her sister.

"The thing out in the crater is the same thing that attacked the settlements, right?" I prompted. Leena nodded. "Well, it's also the same creature that somehow planted vines inside the sorvuc."

"But the vines were completely separate entities,

weren't they? The sorvuc bodies weren't connected by a single parent vine that trailed off and somehow connected back to the creature in the crater?" Leena asked with an intense look on her face.

"No," I replied. "All of the sorvuc were completely separated from each other. However, each cluster of vines woke up at the same moment and started dragging the sorvuc bodies away at the same time."

"What do you mean 'woke up'?" Leena asked.

"The vines didn't look alive at first. They were just there, coiled up. I thought they were dead, too, until one grabbed me," I said.

"If what you're saying is true-"

"It is," I insisted. "It means that the invasive vines might not be just a part of the same species as the creature in the crater, but are possibly somehow part of the creature itself. It's all one entity, that has... what, multiple bodies?"

"An entity that can, apparently, be in multiple places at once," Leena huffed and ran a hand through her ice-blonde hair. "Just what we needed."

"How are we supposed to protect people from something like that?" Mariella gasped.

"How are we supposed to kill something like that?" Leena added.

"We can't kill it," I replied. "This thing, whatever it is, is deeply ingrained in the environment. Until we know how deeply, we can't hurt it. It could be disastrous for us."

"Annie said the same thing," Leena laughed dryly.

"Then you know I'm right."

"But then what the hell do we do?"

ROKUL

Last night, I found every excuse to hang around work with the hope of catching Tella when she left the lab. However, by the time the rest of the personnel started leaving for the night, Tella still hadn't reappeared.

I ran out of reasons to linger and I didn't have an excuse to stay when my brother asked if I was ready to go back to our place.

I suspected Takar knew I was stalling. He gave me that *look*.

It wasn't that I wanted to hide my feelings for Tella, or that I had any problem with my brother knowing I had feelings for a human female.

I simply felt that telling other people was something I shouldn't do without making sure Tella approved.

After all, we hadn't defined the parameters of our relationship. I didn't want to tell Takar something only for it not to be true. It was obvious to me that Tella appreciated her privacy, as well.

I didn't want to violate that.

So Takar and I went back to our place and I had to be content with the possibility of seeing Tella the following morning.

In the morning, Takar woke me up after the alert from my comm unit failed to do so.

"Get up." He tapped me on the forehead. "How can you sleep through that? I can hear it in my room."

"Now I know why you're in such a foul temper all the time. You never get any sleep." I silenced the alert and checked my comm unit. It was a broadcasted message from General Rouhr instructing us to prepare for a meeting in one hour.

"That alert came in ten minutes ago," Takar informed me. "And I'm in a foul mood all the time because you prevent me from getting sleep," he shot back. "Get dressed."

"I'm the eldest. I'm supposed to be the leader," I called after him as he walked back to his room. He didn't say anything, but lifted his hand and made a rude gesture that made me burst out laughing.

Many people assumed Takar and I didn't get along because of the way we interacted with each other. The truth was, we were two halves of one whole being. We balanced each other perfectly. That's why General Rouhr kept us in the same strike team. We weren't as effective when we were in separate teams.

Takar practically dragged me out of our rented rooms twenty minutes later. He hated to be late. The funny thing about Takar was that he considered arriving on time to be arriving late. He liked to arrive ten minutes before the event began. I, on the other hand, if left to my own devices, was always ten minutes late.

We strolled into General Rouhr's conference room precisely on time. Tella was already there. When we locked eyes, she smiled. It was subtle, barely a tug at the corner of her mouth, but it was warm. I smiled back, less subtly than she had.

"Good morning," General Rouhr began. "I've called this meeting so all strike teams can be collectively updated on recent finding concerning our new friend out in the crater."

I looked around the room. Only Vrehx wasn't present. I assumed he was with Jeneva. Dr. Parker, the geologist, was here, as well as Leena. Vidia was here, of course. She was always present at General Rouhr's briefings. She said it was because she liked to keep abreast of the issues the *Vengeance* crew faced, and she needed to know what might affect the human population, but everyone knew it was also because she wanted to be near her mate.

General Rouhr nodded for Tella to present her findings. Tella stood from her seat and moved to where General Rouhr stood.

"I won't bore you with the scientific details," she began, eliciting a round of soft laughter from her audience. "I've found significant evidence that whatever that thing is out in the desert can control other species of sentient plants using invasive, parasitic vines that don't have to be physically connected to the creature to take control of the host."

"The creature has vine minions?" Karzin asked.

"Not exactly," Tella replied. "The parasitic vines are more like clones of the creature itself. Genetic analysis proves it."

I knew something was wrong with those vines, but I wouldn't have guessed they were an extension of the creature itself. The way those vines dragged the sorvuc bodies deeper into the forest showed intelligence

Those vines didn't want Tella to look at the sorvuc bodies.

Now that she'd figured out they were part of the creature, it was obvious we were in more danger than we'd realized.

"What's the next step?" Takar asked.

"Isn't it obvious?" I asked. "If that thing can control

other sentient plants, then we have to remove the sentient plants. Take away its advantage."

"We can't do that." Tella gave me a surprised look that I didn't understand. What other option did we have? "The sentient plant population is vital to maintaining the balance of the forest we rely on for eighty percent of our resources. I'm sure Dr. Parker has already said as much."

"I have," Annie spoke up.

"That was when the creature posed a threat we couldn't do anything about," I replied. "We had no way of stopping the attacks on the settlements. No one remembered them and they happened without warning. Now we have a threat we can stop, so I think we should stop it." My words elicited murmurs of support.

"What you're proposing is a band-aid solution, at best," Tella argued. "Within months the ecosystem will collapse and we'll be in a far worse position than we are now."

"With all due respect, our job is to protect human lives," I said. "If we have the opportunity to do that, you can't ask us not to."

"It's a moot point if the lives you save now are lost in a few weeks because we've destroyed the environment we live in," Tella said. "Do you know what will happen if the sentient plant species die out? The populations of the creatures they feed on will skyrocket. If those populations skyrocket, they'll continue to grow out of control. The forest won't be able to support large increases in population like that. It will collapse and we will collapse with it."

"Then we maintain the environment ourselves," I shrugged.

"How are you going to do that?" Tella challenged, throwing her hands in the air. "This isn't your native world. You don't know enough about the complex ecological structure to manually maintain it, even if it were possible."

"That's why we have experts," I grinned, which only seemed to make Tella more irritated.

"Those experts won't do you much good if you refuse to listen to them," Tella said pointedly.

"That creature out there has already done considerable environmental damage," I pointed out. "If they can control other species of sentient plants, won't that damage the environment just as much as we would if we hunted down the sentient plants? Either way, the sentient plant population will be damaged. Why not save lives in the process?"

"The damage you want to do isn't reversible," Tella countered. "We don't know that the creature in the desert permanently damages the sentient plants it takes control of."

"We can't keep using the fact that we don't know enough about that thing as an excuse to continue doing nothing." I realized I had stood up. I wasn't sure when that happened, but with each word exchanged, Tella and I stepped closer to each other.

"And we can't jump at the first solution without ensuring that it's the best solution," Tella argued. "With all that's at stake, we have to think things through."

"Someone get in between them before they come to blows," Sk'lar interrupted.

"Yes, I think we ought to step back from this issue," General Rouhr cut in.

Tella returned to her seat without another glance in my direction.

"You both make fair points," General Rouhr continued. "However, Rokul is right when he says our duty is to save lives."

"At least give me a chance to find an alternative," Tella suggested.

"Us," Leena jumped in, surprising us all. "Give *us* a chance to find an alternative."

"Such as?" General Rouhr lifted a brow in interest.

"A neutralizer or a tranquilizer," Tella blurted. "Something that will kill the vines without killing the main body of the sentient plant."

General Rouhr fell silent as he considered his options. After a moment, he looked to Vidia, who nodded ever so subtly to Tella and Leena. With that nod, I knew my suggestion was out the window.

"You have three days to come up with something," General Rouhr instructed Leena and Tella. "If you don't have a viable plan by then, we'll have to go with Rokul's plan."

"Yes, sir," Tella murmured.

"Thank you, General," Leena added with a smile.

"I hope you can pull it off," General Rouhr replied. He turned to face the rest of us. "If there are no other concerns, you're all dismissed. Go about your regular duties."

I wanted to talk to Tella, but she refused to meet my gaze. She looked furious.

As soon as she had the chance, she slipped out of the room without so much as a glance in my direction.

Skrell.

TELLA

I felt Rokul's eyes on me as I stood up. I didn't want to talk to him.

He'd already explained his viewpoint and made it perfectly clear that, no matter what overwhelming evidence I showed him to the contrary, he still believed his plan was the best one.

Who the hell did Rokul think he was?

Did my years of schooling and experience mean nothing?

Was I unclear at any point?

Or was Rokul just too eager to pick up a blaster and charge into battle to listen to anything I said?

I wiggled past the other aliens trying to leave the conference room. I didn't want to be near anyone right now. Once free of the crowd, I stormed off to the lab.

Perhaps there was something else I could use that would convince Rokul beyond a shadow of a doubt that killing all of the sentient plants was the wrong way to go.

I fought the urge to break something. My mother always told me my temper was my one vice. Of course, I had plenty of other vices when she'd told me that. She just didn't know about them.

I paced the walkways between the lab stations. While I paced, I heard someone enter the room. I assumed it was Rokul, so I looked up, teeth bared and ready to argue.

Leena laughed when she saw my expression.

"If you're looking for round two, you'll have to go somewhere else," she joked. I sighed and pressed the palm of my hand into my forehead.

"I'm sorry. I thought you were Rokul," I explained.

"I assumed so," Leena said. "We aren't the best of friends, but I don't think I've done anything to warrant that kind of look from you."

"No, you haven't," I smiled weakly. "Thanks for having my back in that meeting."

"Of course," Leena grinned. "You're the one in the right."

"Rokul doesn't think so," I huffed.

"Fuck him," Leena shrugged.

I almost did, I thought to myself.

"I just can't believe that after seeing me in action on multiple occasions, knowing my qualifications, and the fact that his general brought me in because I'm an expert, Rokul had the audacity to think he knew better than me!" I threw my hands up as a fresh wave of anger hit me.

"That's just how men are," Leena smirked.

"He's not a man. He's a Skotan." I rolled my eyes.

"He might be a different species but all males have some universal similarities," Leena replied with a smirk.

"Then what good are they?" I exclaimed, but I started laughing before I could finish the sentence.

"We know what they're good for," Leena winked.

"Rokul could be good for that. Not that I would know," I added quickly. "But I don't know if I can get past what happened in there."

"Skotan are extremely military oriented, more so than the other races," Leena explained. "It's in his nature to say things like that."

"I understand that," I replied, and I did. "But he and I are supposed to be friends. If he can't respect my educated, professional opinion, how can I trust him to respect any of my other opinions?"

"You mean like in a personal way?" Leena asked.

"Yes," I clarified. "Friendship is built on trust and respect. If I don't trust him to respect me, then we can't be friends."

"I suppose you have your answer, then." Leena gave me a sympathetic look.

"I guess so." A frown tugged at the corners of my mouth.

Rokul and I were on our way to becoming more than friends, but that wasn't something I wanted to share with Leena. Especially now.

"Don't take it so hard," Leena smiled encouragingly. "Friendships are full of pitfalls. Let's talk about our new assignment to take your mind off it."

"That sounds perfect," I said gratefully. "Any thoughts?"

"I liked your idea of a neutralizer," Leena said.

"I said something about a neutralizer?" I asked, brow furrowed.

"Yes. Rouhr asked you for alternate suggestions and that's what you said," Leena explained.

"I was so pissed off, I didn't realize I even said anything," I replied.

"Wow," Leena chuckled. "Maybe you should work on that."

"Excuse me," I laughed. "You were the angriest, most unpleasant person in our lab at the university."

"Exactly! I know what I'm talking about. Take my advice," she replied.

"Good point," I nodded.

"If you thought I was so angry and unpleasant, why did you talk to me?" Leena asked.

"Because you were the least insufferable person there," I replied honestly.

"That's why I talked to you, too," Leena replied. "I still always thought you were some stuck -up goody-goody. Looks like I was mistaken. You've got some bite to you."

Back then, I had been a goody-goody. I didn't want to tell Leena that losing my parents and sister was what put this bite in me.

I didn't want her to look at me with pity.

"You okay?" Leena asked. I blinked, snapping myself back to the here and now. Though my attention returned to Leena, my heart continued to ache with a familiar pain that would never fully go away.

"Yeah," I said a little too brightly. "I think a neutralizer is the right way to go."

"So do I. That leaves us with two possible options. We can create something that will simply render the creature in question unconscious, or we can create something that will specifically target the invasive vines," Leena explained.

"Considering we only have three days, I think we should focus on making a simple tranquilizer," I decided. "Once General Rouhr allows us more time, we can come up with something that will harm the invasive vines, but not the host creature."

"Makes sense," Leena nodded. "I can make the tranquilizer if you tell me what to put in it."

"That's where it gets a little tricky," I said. "I've seen those vines inside two separate species of plant. I've never tried to tranq a sorvuc or a kodanos. I don't know if a tranquilizer that works on one will work on the other. Also, I don't know how many other sentient plant species are susceptible to the invasive vines or if non-sentient plants are at risk, too."

"Let's focus on the sentient plants first," Leena suggested. "Sorvuc are the only species of sentient plant that we know those vines invaded for the purpose of harming a human settlement."

"Right," I nodded. "Ideally, I'd like to develop a way to extract the vines from the unconscious sorvuc without harming it."

"One step at a time," Leena cautioned. "We'll worry about that once we make a decent tranquilizer. I assume you'll have no problem going out into the field to test these yourself?"

"Not at all," I almost smiled, but not quite. Yes, I was anxious to get back in the field where I didn't have to think about anything other than completing the job I'd been given.

The catch was, General Rouhr wouldn't let me go

out into the field alone, and I'd already made such a fuss over only wanting Rokul to be my guard.

Rokul was the last person I wanted to be out in the field with right now. Thinking about him made me feel angry all over again.

This time, I wasn't angry about what Rokul had said during the meeting, but that I'd allowed him to take up so much space in my head in the first place.

"Hello?" Leena exclaimed. Her elevated voice made me flinch.

"What?" I asked.

"You didn't hear a word I said, did you?" Leena asked with a knowing smile.

"I'm sorry," I sighed. "I'm having trouble focusing."

"Obviously," Leena rolled her eyes.

"What were you saying?" I asked.

"I think you should take the rest of the day off," she urged. "I can put together a few basic, pesticide-based neutralizers without you. You can come in tomorrow and tweak them."

I almost insisted that I was fine to work, but a sudden wave of exhaustion washed over me. I realized that I'd been going nonstop since before I arrived in Rigkon.

"Yeah, I think I'll do that," I nodded. Leena looked relieved.

"Good," she smiled. "I don't have time to repeat myself over and over." I laughed dryly.

"I'll be in tomorrow morning," I informed her.

"I'll have something for you to work with by then," Leena assured me.

I kept my head down as I walked out of the lab. The last thing I wanted was to run into Rokul. Luckily, I made it out of the building without anyone taking notice.

The Blooming Bud, where I rented my room, was a short walk from General Rouhr's building. I felt tempted to stop by Dr. Hines's lab and do some of the mind-numbing work I'd been hired to do. If I did that, I could go to bed tonight feeling like I'd done something productive.

Instead, I walked into the first tavern I spotted.

ROKUL

"Rokul!" Takar snapped his fingers in front of my face. I flinched and, purely out of instinct, lifted one arm into a defensive position, the other fist pulled back to throw.

"What?" I snapped at my brother.

"You've been scowling at the table for the last ten minutes. Are you going to help me with this or not?" Takar gestured to the table full of weapons we needed to clean that day.

"If by help you mean redo everything you do wrong, then yes." I picked up a standard issue blaster and dismantled it for proper cleaning.

"You wouldn't know how to clean anything if it weren't for me," Takar scoffed. "In fact, you wouldn't know how to enable passive mode on your blaster if it weren't for me."

"I still don't understand why anyone needs a passive mode. If you're carrying a blaster, I assume you're planning on using it," I replied.

"Some don't fancy the idea of a blaster going off in their supply pack," Takar said.

"Why would someone carry a blaster in a supply pack?" I wondered.

"Why would someone glare at a wall instead of apologizing to the human female they angered?" Takar replied.

"I don't know what you're talking about."

"You attacked her credibility in front of everyone," Takar continued as if I hadn't said anything.

"That wasn't my intention." I dropped the act. I knew I couldn't lie to Takar. He knew me too well. "I simply felt like she wasn't looking at our situation from a military perspective."

"Why do you think General Rouhr brought her in?" Takar asked.

"To acquire information about the creature in the desert," I replied.

"Which is exactly what she did," Takar continued. "If General Rouhr wanted to approach this problem from only a military point of view, we would've dropped grenades on that thing by now."

"I still don't understand why we haven't done exactly that," I said.

"Tella explained it to us. Annie Parker explained it to us. If you still don't understand, then I suggest you locate Tella and ask her to explain it to you again. And apologize while you're at it," Takar replied.

"You're right," I sighed. "I still think my plan makes more sense, however, I shouldn't have undermined her in front of everyone. I'm going to go find her."

"You're not leaving me with all the work," Takar said sternly. I looked at the tableful of weapons. At this rate, I wouldn't be out of here until after sundown. Maybe it was better that way. It would allow Tella some time to calm down.

"Fine," I nodded and returned to the blaster I'd begun to clean. I burned through exactly half of the weapons on the table in record time. If I hurried, I could still catch Tella in the lab before she left for the day.

"I've done half. I'd say that's fair," I said to Takar.

"I watched you rush through them. They'll need to be rechecked." Takar gave me a disapproving stare.

"I really need to make things right with Tella and I can't stay," I said. "I'll owe you." Takar considered my offer for a few moments.

"Do all of my reports for the rest of the week," Takar said.

"Deal." I hurried out of the armory and didn't stop until I reached the lab. I was relieved to see there was still a light on inside.

"Tella," I called as I pushed my way into the lab.

"Nope," Leena said without looking up from her station. "She took an early day."

"Oh," I frowned. "Is she all right?"

"She's pissed at you," Leena smirked. I considered Leena a friend more so than I did the other human women. I enjoyed her dry sense of humor and her straightforward way of thinking. I could always count on the truth from Leena.

Including right now.

"What should I do?" I asked.

"Isn't that obvious?" She looked up from her workstation, one eyebrow raised.

"I'm already planning on apologizing," I assured her. "But I'd like to know the best way to do that."

"Admit you were acting like a narrow-minded idiot?" Leena suggested.

"If that's what it takes, I'll do it," I replied.

"You really like her, don't you?" Leena gave me a knowing look.

"Is it that obvious?" I asked.

"You're willing to set your dignity aside to ensure her forgiveness. No offense, but that's not exactly in character for you," Leena replied.

"No offense taken," I said. "Did Tella go back to the room she's renting?"

"That's what I told her to do," Leena said. "I wouldn't bother her at home, though. She needs time to decompress."

"You're probably right," I admitted. "I'll find her tomorrow. I should think about what I'm going to say in advance."

"That would be a first," Leena snorted.

I left the lab disappointed and made my way back to the armory. Takar was hard at work recleaning all of the weapons.

"I take it back," I said when I entered. "Tella wasn't there. I'll help you finish up."

"No need," Takar replied. "I'd rather have you doing my reports for the week than help me finish this."

"You're joking."

"Not at all," Takar replied. "I'm enjoying the peace that comes with maintaining the weapons."

"Right," I said slowly. Sometimes I couldn't believe Takar and I were related.

"This is the part where you leave me in peace," Takar urged.

"If that's what you want. Enjoy your peace."

With nothing else to do, I decided I might as well head back to my place. I walked slowly, thinking about Tella and everything I wanted to say to her. I didn't pick up my pace even as it began to rain. I couldn't remember the last time it had rained here. I enjoyed the feeling of wet droplets on my skin.

As I walked, a warm-looking tavern caught my eye. At that moment, I realized I wanted nothing more than a drink. I entered the tavern, pausing in the doorway to wipe the grime of the city off the soles of my boots. I looked around the tavern. I wasn't surprised to see that it was mostly empty.

A few people sat at the bar, chatting amiably. A single woman sat at a booth. A woman I knew.

Tella sat with her head dipped. She had one drink in front of her but it looked like she had yet to take a sip. As she sat, unaware that she was being watched, I got a glimpse of her face.

She looked worn down. Her shoulders were hunched. I could see the dark circles under her eyes from here.

It hit me like a fist. I'd done that. I was supposed to protect her. Keep her safe.

And I'd done this, instead.

I walked over to her booth.

"Is that seat taken?" I asked quietly.

Tella jumped slightly and looked up. Her expression hardened, but she jerked her chin, indicating that I was allowed to take a seat. I slid into the booth across from her.

"I'd like to apologize," I said quickly. Tella lifted her brows in surprise but didn't say anything. "I shouldn't have challenged your expertise in front of everyone."

"That isn't why I'm upset," Tella said. "I don't care that it was in front of everyone. I'm upset because, despite my experience, you felt that you knew better than me. I felt incredibly disrespected. I can't be friends, or more than friends, with someone who doesn't respect me."

"I don't think you realize how much respect I have for you," I said. "I've never met anyone, human, alien, male or female, who can keep up with me the way you can. In fact, when I first met you, I found myself keeping up with *you*."

"Then why did you treat me like I didn't know what I was talking about?" Tella asked.

"I get too caught up in finding fast solutions," I explained. "Takar tells me all the time that I don't stop to consider consequences enough. He's right."

"Your plan wasn't completely ridiculous," Tella offered. "In a more stable environment, I would've agreed with your plan."

"But it's not a stable environment. You and Annie have both told us that before. The Skota Capulus is an almost unshakeable environment. It's mostly red-rock desert," I continued. "It's difficult for me to conceptualize an environmental collapse since I've never lived on a planet where that's a possibility until now."

"You've never mentioned your homeworld before." Tella tipped her head to one side.

Her eyes looked into mine and there was a shift inside me. I swallowed.

"None of us like to talk about our homeworlds," I admitted. "We're all still coming to terms with the fact that we might never see them again."

Tella bit her bottom lip.

"I never thought about that," she said quietly. "Should I not ask about it?" She tilted her head again.

I had the urge to touch her face in that moment.

"It's okay," I smiled, hoping warmth crept into my voice. "Takar and I are lucky. We have each other. No one else has had contact with any of their family members since we fell through the rift."

"You *are* lucky," Tella said. "I lost my entire family during the Xathi invasion."

I felt my heart drop.

"I'm so sorry." I reached across the table and laid my hand atop hers. She didn't pull away. I didn't want to say it out loud, but a lot of things about her started to make sense.

"It's fine," she said quietly.

"No, it isn't. Nothing the Xathi did to us is fine," I replied.

Tella stared at the table, discomfort radiating from her small body.

Desperate to keep her from shutting down on me when I was feeling closer to her, I came up with a plan.

"Can I buy you a drink?"

"I already have one," Tella replied with a faint smile. Her eyes twinkled at me and I knew not all hope was lost.

"How about dinner, then?" I offered. I smiled widely at her.

She lifted her head and looked me over.

"Dinner?"

"Dinner."

I watched her suck in her lower lip and meet my gaze again.

I wasn't sure what she was looking for, but she must've found it.

"Yes, I'll have dinner with you," she agreed.

My heart rose anew. Tella was a woman like no other. I laced my fingers with hers.

"I know our past is dark," I started, then caught myself. Serious conversation wasn't exactly what I was known for. But I couldn't exactly ask Takar for help on this. "But my future is brighter with you in it, Tella." I let myself taste her name as I said it.

She smiled, just a tiny bit, just enough to make my

heart leap in my chest as she leaned closer to me. "And so is mine with you, Rokul." Her cheeks flushed.

I liked having that effect on her.

TELLA

I was nervous at first. I didn't know how to act around Rokul without having work as a buffer. I'd really have preferred to be in the field, with something trying to kill us.

Instead, we just talked.

Not about his homeworld or my family at all, which I was fine with. Now that he knew, I expected him to give me that certain look I hated. He did, but only for a moment. He understood that pity wasn't helpful.

He told me about some of the ridiculous things he'd done during his impressive military career. Those stories usually ended in Rokul's brother stepping in before Rokul ended up dead.

"Next time I see your brother, I'm going to offer him my condolences," I joked.

"What's that supposed to mean?" Rokul laughed.

"It means you've probably taken thirty years off his life," I replied.

"Impossible. He was born an old Skotan," he chuckled. "Besides, I think he likes swooping in and being the voice of reason. It makes him feel smart."

"You don't like feeling smart?" I asked.

"I'm not stupid, it's just that I think it makes more sense to be effective than worry about coming off as super-intelligent," he explained. "I like knowing that I've done my job and made a difference."

"Even if you recklessly endanger yourself in the process?" I asked.

"You're one to talk," Rokul replied. "In case you've forgotten, the first time I saw you was when you were suspended by your ankles over the mouth of a carnivorous flower. You don't get to scold me about reckless endangerment when you're just as bad about it as I am."

"I'm still mad at you for killing the Helmria Ithalma," I replied.

"It was going to eat you!" Rokul exclaimed.

"It's a critically endangered species," I said.

"Like I said, you have no room to talk," he laughed.

Our food was placed in front of us, halting conversation for the time being. I hadn't eaten anything that day. I hadn't realized how hungry I was. I had a bad habit of delaying meals or skipping them altogether when I was really focused on a project. I cleaned my plate before Rokul was halfway through his.

"This is what I meant when I said you're the first person I've had to try to keep up with," Rokul laughed between bites. I sipped a glass of water as he finished his meal. I'd finished my drink before we got our food, but I felt no need to order another one.

Rokul paid our tab when we finished our meal.

"I'll walk you back to your place," he offered.

"You don't have to," I shrugged. Realizing how I must've sounded, I quickly added, "but I'd like it if you did."

"It would be my pleasure." Rokul opened the door for me, but I stopped short. Outside, it was pouring rain.

"I think I'll take that second drink," I laughed.

"Sorry, we're closing up," the women who'd served us spoke up.

"We can make it in the rain," Rokul grinned. "It'll be fun."

"If you say so," I replied. He took my hand and pulled me out into the rain. Within seconds, my clothing was soaked through.

"This was a terrible idea!" I shouted to Rokul as we

dashed through the empty streets of Nyheim. Everyone else had had the good sense to go indoors.

"This was a great idea!" Rokul called back. "We don't have to fight against civilian foot traffic to get anywhere."

I directed Rokul through the empty streets until we reached the Blooming Bud. The bar was closed for the night, but there was a rusty metal staircase secured to the outside of the building that led up to my rented room.

I fumbled with the key when we got up the stairs.

"Hurry up," Rokul laughed. "I don't think these stairs can hold both of us."

"Not helping." The cold seeped through my skin, making my hands tremble.

"Just let me do it." Rokul plucked the key from my hand and opened my door. I burst inside and immediately went to turn on the heater that had only worked once since I'd moved in the other day.

"Interesting place," Rokul said as he took in the bare-bones room. My single room was furnished with basic, but outdated, kitchen supplies, a couch with several suspicious puncture wounds, and a metal frame bed with a thin mattress and a single blanket.

"It's affordable," I shrugged. "And I just got here."

Rokul sat down on the couch. It groaned under his weight.

"Have you considered getting a permanent place in Nyheim?" he asked.

"I've thought about it," I replied. "Someplace nicer than this, sure. I just don't know if I want to stay here.

"Oh?" Rokul frowned.

"I don't feel like working in Dr. Hines's lab is right for me." I took a seat on the couch beside him and hoped it wouldn't break. I didn't want to pay for damages. "I can handle working in labs if I have ample opportunity to be in the field, but Dr. Hines isn't going to let me do that for a while. And if she does eventually let me do field projects, it'll be done under her name, since it's her lab."

"That doesn't seem right," Rokul frowned.

"Technically, all of my projects would be her projects, since she'd be the one funding them. That's just how it is," I shrugged.

"I can see why you've never liked working in labs," Rokul replied. "Does that mean all of Annie's work with the soil samples belongs to Dr. Hines?"

"Annie got lucky," I said. "She discovered everything by accident and most of the work on the soil samples wasn't done in Dr. Hines's lab. Annie will get credit for everything if she publishes her findings, unless General Rouhr claims it."

"He wouldn't do that," Rokul said. "I doubt he even realizes he could do that."

"He doesn't seem like the sort that would pull something like that," I agreed. "That's why I don't mind working for him."

"Leena certainly likes having you around," Rokul chuckled. "When we all lived together on the *Aurora*, Leena shared the lab with others. Now, everyone's scattered. Her sister temporarily relocated to Glymna and Jeneva's confined to her bed until she has her child. Dr. Evie Parr is the only other human woman who's consistently in the building with her, though they work in different areas."

"Glad I could be there for her," I said because I didn't know what else to say.

"If you were to leave after completing your work for General Rouhr, I think Leena would be lonely." Rokul nodded seriously. "I think she would miss you."

"It's not like I'd never visit," I laughed. "And I think Leena is more than capable of managing a healthy social life."

"Leena isn't the only one who would mind," Rokul muttered.

"Oh?" I smiled slyly. "Who else would miss me when I leave?"

"I would," Rokul said without hesitation. A pleasant shiver ran up my spine.

"I'd miss you, too," I admitted.

"I can't see you working in a lab day in and day out. An exciting life in exciting places would suit you," Rokul grinned. "But I hope you'd always come back to visit between projects."

"Yes, I would," I smiled. "Someone has to make sure you don't drive you brother insane."

"Oh, I'm going to drive him insane whether or not you come to visit," Rokul joked. As we spoke, we slowly angled our bodies to face each other. His smile was infectious and warmth radiated off him, drawing me in closer.

I shivered, painfully aware of the throb in my skin caused not just by cold, but by arousal. Rokul was so close. The time I thought might never come was at hand.

I wanted him to tear my clothes off and warm me up with his mouth. That mouth that had forever changed me with a kiss.

My thoughts were uncontrollable, and I didn't have to worry about my body. Rokul was there, on me.

"You need to get out of those clothes." Rokul slung his arm around my shoulders and pulled me close in an effort to get to me stop shivering.

Surrendering to my urge to touch him, I tucked my head into the crook of his neck in an attempt to absorb as much heat as possible.

As he held me, I lifted my chin to look up at him. I found him looking down at me with a warm, almost sleepy look in his eyes.

I wasn't sure who moved first. I might've lifted my head up to him or he might've lowered his head down to me. That didn't matter. All that mattered was the moment when our lips touched.

I felt every part of my body relax against his. He held me closer. I was content to let him take control of the moment. I needed him to show me how to do this.

He cupped the base of my head in one large, warm hand. My hand slid up his chest. I could feel his heartbeat against my fingertips.

The only things that existed anymore were his hands, his warmth, and his lips.

In that moment, I utterly belonged to him. My hands ran up and down his body, and his mine. It wasn't just about warmth. It was about need. We both had it, and we would both obey it now.

Nothing could stop us.

A clap of thunder caused me to flinch, breaking the spell.

Okay, a big loud cracking sound making me jump did shake things up a bit.

"It sounds like it's whipping up into a proper storm," Rokul observed. There was a thickness to his voice that I knew must be the lust we both shared.

"It's been a proper storm," I agreed. My hand pressed more firmly against him, saying in touch what I couldn't with words as I continued. "It's getting late and that rain isn't going to let up any time soon. Why don't you just stay here for the night?"

"Are you alright with that?" Rokul asked. There was that dark, delicious quality in his voice that sent tingles to my brain stem. I wanted him so much.

"If I wasn't, I wouldn't have offered. I'm not a naturally hospitable person," I laughed, a little nervously.

It also pressed my breasts against him, which I craved. I wanted to feel him on me, all over me. Desire didn't have any logic to it, it was just one instinct overtaking another. My lips and my lust weren't connected in the slightest.

"Shocking," he joked.

Rokul respectfully turned around while I changed out of my wet clothes.

I tugged on an old shirt and a pair of soft sleeping pants. When I faced him, he'd taken off his own shirt. I tried not to stare at the broad, well-shaped expanse of his chest, but I couldn't help myself. He didn't seem to mind my gaze.

"I'm not sure I'm going to fit on the couch." He frowned.

"Share the bed with me," I blurted out. A blush crept up my cheeks. Oh god. Had I really said that out loud?

Rokul froze.

"Only if you don't mind."

I shook my head. "I wouldn't have offered if I minded."

He strode over to the bed and removed his soaked pants, revealing fitted black shorts underneath. He climbed into bed and made himself comfortable before pulling back the covers for me.

I climbed in next to him, leaving a few inches of space between us. Rokul wrapped an arm around me and pulled me against him. I let myself curl into his warm body.

"I won't let you freeze," he joked.

"Too late." I pressed my ice-cold hands against his bare chest. His skin felt like fire.

"Skrell!" he swore as he covered my hand with his. "That can't be healthy."

"It's fine," I laughed. "I'll warm up in a little while."

"I'll make sure of that." Rokul moved so that most of my body was in contact with his.

The overwhelmingly delicious sensations of his body against mine were a heady mix, a refuge from reality as I focused intently on just the sensations. The masculine scent of him. The sound of his heartbeat. The movement of his breathing.

The way he held me.

The cold didn't stand a chance, because the joy in this moment was bone-deep.

As I started to warm up, we fell asleep listening to the sound of the rain.

ROKUL

There was this terrible tingling in my arm that woke me up. As I lay there, groggy and yawning, I realized that I couldn't move my arm, something had it pinned.

I took a second to remember where I was and who I was with, and I grinned.

Somehow, Tella had ended up using my arm as a pillow, and now I was paying for it.

I ever so gently pulled my arm from under her head, not an easy thing to do, and upon my release, climbed out of bed and started rubbing my arm and shaking my hand. It was excruciating for a couple of minutes, but eventually full blood flow returned, and I was back to normal.

This was a price I'd gladly pay again and again. It

felt incredibly calming and soothing to have her sleep in my arms. It was a sense of belonging like I had never felt before -- she seemed to fit there exactly and I found myself shutting my eyes for a moment to recall the scent of her hair, the rise and fall of her chest.

I looked back at Tella's sleeping form and wondered what Takar would say to my having feelings for a human woman.

This... might not be good.

He would probably chastise me for it. While we had both admitted that the human females were attractive, at least some of them, we had originally made fun of Vrehx and Axtin for falling for them.

And here I was, doing the same thing.

It wasn't just the physical parts of Tella that appealed to me, although I was determined to study her body more closely and much more often. It was her mind that drew me in, as well.

The idea that she was so willing to study something no one else had an interest in, that intrigued me.

The fact that she presented herself as such an independent woman that could fend for herself piqued my interest.

The tiny little things she did that counteracted that 'tough girl' persona held my curiosity.

There was so much to Tella that I didn't know, and I

found myself wanting to know more about her every minute, every second, every breath of the day.

I quietly chuckled to myself as I moved to the far side of the room so I wouldn't disturb her. I began my morning exercises and tried to stay as quiet as possible.

My mind drifted through fantasies of waking her with a kiss. Of waiting for her eyes to recognize mine and then for her lips and legs to part for me. I wanted to claim every inch of her with my mouth and tongue, with my hands, to reinforce my possession.

I wanted to whisper something sweet in Tella's ear and pull her tight to me.

I wanted to climb in bed with her and let the blackness of sleep envelop me, perfectly entangled with her, like nothing else mattered.

I couldn't stop thinking about how much she had changed me.

We were similar, Tella and I.

And, for the first time in a long time, I had to admit that I was a bit scared.

Not scared. Of course not.

Apprehensive.

What if she didn't feel as strongly for me as I did for her?

It was obvious we were attracted to one another, as evidenced by our time together, but what if I was the one that felt more, and she didn't?

She had already admitted that she wasn't the type to stay in one place. She liked to move around, keep exploring, keep moving, keep active. I respected that. I was similar to her in that aspect.

My only reason for staying in one place for an extended period of time was Takar. The exciting thing about military life was that we moved around, we were rarely in one place for long, so I understood her that way.

As I switched to sit-ups, I wondered about how life would be with her. I could almost guarantee that it would be an adventure, even if we didn't travel all over the planet. Just dinner with her was an adventure, so I could imagine what a lifetime would be like.

Why did I want to be with her so badly? Life in the military was generally solitary, certainly dangerous, and it was guaranteed to shorten your lifespan. That was why you either didn't form connections with too many people, or the connections you did make were stronger than almost anything else.

And that was before the Xathi had attacked.

Now, nothing was certain, and life was short.

If she chose to reciprocate my feelings, I was positive we would be happy, but for how long?

Other than my brother, I had never had a close relationship. What kind of relationships did Tella have in her past?

"Unngh, will you keep it down over there?" I heard Tella moan.

"Sorry," I whispered. Without realizing it, I had worked up a good sweat and must been making too much noise. I settled down and began my stretching exercises as she rolled over in the bed and went back to sleep. Her naked back looked smooth and beautiful, if you looked past her scars.

That was the other thing, what did I know about her?

What if she was the type to be in a relationship but not *be* in a relationship? What if she was interested in enjoying our time together, but was not interested in being exclusive? Could I handle that? Would I be okay with that?

I finished my stretches, went to the small kitchen, and looked for a way to make coffee. At least that was something I knew about humans, they all liked coffee. Not seeing a coffee-maker around, I decided to fake it. I got out a small pot, filled it with water, and put it on the stove to warm up. Then I found a small jar of the powder in the back of a cupboard and coffee filters. I took two filters, filled one with instant coffee, then folded it and tied it up into a modified baggie. I wrapped it in the second filter, tying it off as well. When the water was near boiling, I put the coffee baggie in the pot and watched as it began to steep.

Within minutes, I had a pot of coffee. I got down two mugs from a cupboard and filled them with coffee. I made a small mess, but it was an easy clean-up. I had heard of humans drinking their coffee either black, with sugar, with cream, with ice, with whiskey, or with milk. But I didn't know what Tella had, or what she'd want. I left it untouched, she could add in whatever she wanted.

I brought the coffee to the bed and flipped on the light. With light already coming over the horizon, I figured it would be acceptable to turn on the interior lights and wake her up. She was even more beautiful as she woke up, her hair mussed and covering her face, her overexaggerated moan she let out as she stretched, her perky breasts defying gravity clearly revealed in the thin shirt.

"What are you smiling at?" she asked as she pushed the hair out of her face.

"You. Morning," I answered.

"Did you make coffee?" she asked again as she swung her legs out of bed. She had yet to cover up, so modesty wasn't one of her strong points, at least not with me.

"Yep."

"Why?" she yawned.

I shrugged. "Humans like coffee."

"Huh. Not all humans. I drink it, but only once in a

while. The last renter must have left the fixings for it behind." Her smile took the sting out of her words. "Thanks," she said with a kiss to my cheek while she took the cup.

"I am at your bidding," I said with a promise in my smile.

She smiled and winked back. "Then I'll have to think about something special to ask for."

TELLA

For the first time in a long time, I didn't want to go to work. The coffee Rokul made for me was bitter, but he was so proud of making something that humans like, so I drank it all without complaint.

"I'll make some eggs before we head to work," I offered.

"I've got to stop by the place I share with my brother," Rokul said, standing up. "I'll never hear the end of it if he notices I'm wearing the same clothing two days in a row."

"Would he really care that much that you spent the night with someone?" I asked, suddenly feeling self-conscious.

"No," he smiled and extended a hand to me. "He'll just be overdramatic about how terrible I smell."

"I don't think you smell terrible," I replied.

"Neither do I. But Takar will." Rokul stepped around the tiny table that served as my dining table to kiss me on the cheek. "I'll see you in a little while."

His lips were still close to my cheek where he'd kissed me, and I turned so I could feel his warm breath on my lips. Our eyes locked and the little space remaining between us disappeared, him pulling me close to him and my lips parting. His tongue swept over mine and I moaned into his mouth.

I wanted the taste of him to linger in my mouth all day, long after he left. Watching him leave, I felt a reverie wash over me of the feeling of sleeping in his arms. It was perfect.

After he left, I decided to make myself some breakfast anyway. Usually, I wasn't hungry in the mornings. Often, it would be late afternoon by the time I had my first meal. This morning, I was ravenous. I fried up three eggs and ate them right out of the pan.

Now that Rokul had left, my place felt colder. He was officially more effective than the heater my room came with. I stepped into the shower and turned up the water as hot as it would go until I could feel my fingers and toes once more.

The rain had stopped sometime in the night. The streets were mostly dry, with a few puddles here and there. All of the buildings looked clean and refreshed. I felt clean and refreshed, too, as I walked to General Rouhr's building.

Though he'd left my rented space over an hour ago, I still felt Rokul's skin against mine. Wherever he went, he left his warmth behind him like the fading sun. I felt happy to linger in that tail when he wasn't with me.

I was so caught up in my memories of Rokul that I walked right past General Rouhr's building. Only the Valorni guard stationed at the door noticed, barely bothering to hide a smile as I walked back.

Leena was already hard at work when I strolled into the lab.

"Do you ever go home?" I asked her.

"I got here at the same time you usually get here," Leena replied. When she looked up from her station, she gave me a once over. "You look oddly glowy. Did you get laid last night?"

"Excuse me?" I choked on the words.

"Oh my god, you did!" Leena gasped. "When I told you to go back to your place and lie down, I didn't think you'd bring someone with you!"

"I didn't get laid!" I shrieked.

"Then why do you have that look on your face?" Leena asked. "Don't try to tell me it was a good night's sleep. I don't care if your bed is made out of clouds and Lidwig feathers. No amount of sleep results in that transformation." She gestured broadly to me.

"I did get a good night's sleep," I insisted. "Not because I got laid, but because I had someone next to me to keep me warm."

"You had someone in your bed with you all night and you didn't fuck them?" Leena looked at me as if I'd just slapped her sister. "Who was it?"

"I'm not going to tell you that," I blushed.

"It was Rokul," Leena said with a knowing nod.

"You can't know that and I'm not telling," I repeated.

"Who else would it be?" Leena shrugged. "You only know me and Rokul in this building."

"I know more people than that," I said a little defensively.

"What's the name of the Valorni guarding the entrance this morning?" Leena asked.

"I don't know. I've never seen him before," I replied.

"Yes, you have. He's there every other day," Leena said smugly.

"Now you're making me feel like an asshole," I muttered.

"Just admit it was Rokul you spent the night with and I'll stop making you feel like an asshole," Leena grinned triumphantly.

"Fine, it was Rokul." I threw my hands up. "Tell me the name of the Valorni at the front door."

"Oh, I have no idea. I've never seen him before,"

Leena smirked. "I said hello to him when I came in, though."

"I can't believe I fell for that." I shook my head.

"I can't believe you spent the night with Rokul and didn't have sex with him," Leena grinned. "You must have some insane self-control."

"Believe me, I considered it. But I really did need sleep. I think he did, too." I smiled fondly at the memory.

"It's not as fun to talk about when you're not embarrassed about it," Leena teased. "Do you want to see what I did yesterday after you left?"

"Absolutely." I knew I wouldn't be able to put Rokul completely out of my mind today, or ever again. However, there was still the mystery plant and its invasive vines to deal with.

"It's nothing fancy." Leena laid out three small vials filled with identical amounts of clear liquid. Each one was marked with a different percentage. "I altered the composition of one of the common pesticides on the market so it targets brain activity rather than vital organs and systems."

"Oh, is that all?"

"Well, the sentient plants don't have traditional brains, organs, and systems, so I had to tweak it more than I'd planned," Leena continued. "I ran the compound through a few different simulations. That's how I got these values." Leena indicated the percentages marked on the vials.

"Those three concentrations yielded good results?"

"Yes. However, the simulation isn't exact, nor is it foolproof. All three of these should have the desired effect, but they need to be tested on actual sentient plants," Leena said. My face lit up.

"I'm more than happy to test them," I said not caring if I sounded overeager.

"Not surprising. Go talk to General Rouhr," Leena instructed.

I hurried out of the lab with a new spring in my step. General Rouhr was in his office, as usual, scrolling through a datapad with a tired expression on his face. To my surprise, Councilwoman Vidia was in the office, as well. She stood behind the general's chair, reading over the top of his head and rubbing his shoulders.

Not knowing what else to do, I cleared my throat. General Rouhr looked up from his datapad with a curious expression.

"Dr. Briar," he smiled when he recognized me. "Can I help you?"

"Dr. Dewitt's developed three potential neutralizers to use against sentient plants under the control of invasive vines," I explained. "I'd like permission to test them in the field."

"Not on your own." General Rouhr spoke in a way that reminded me of my father, serious yet concerned.

"Of course not," I assured him.

"Do you want to take Rokul?" General Rouhr offered. I tried to smother a smile at the phrasing of the question.

"If that's all right with you, General." I managed to reply with no hint of humor in my voice.

"He's all yours," General Rouhr replied.

"Thank you. I'll get the results to you as soon as I have them." General Rouhr nodded and went back to his datapad. Councilwoman Vidia offered me a kind smile. I left his office feeling lighter than air. I was so excited to find Rokul and tell him we had a new assignment.

As I walked through the corridors, it occurred to me that I hadn't been this excited to see another living being in a long time. If it weren't for the odd stares I'd attract, I would run through the hallways in order to find Rokul faster.

Damn, I was smitten.

How the hell did that happen?

I wasn't sure where to go to find Rokul. I hardly spent time outside of the lab. I thought I was walking in the direction of the armory when I spotted Rokul's brother.

"Takar!" I called as I caught up to him. He looked

down at me, only the faintest glimmer of recognition in his eyes. "I'm looking for Rokul, have you seen him?" I asked.

"He was late this morning," Takar said. "I assume you had something to do with that."

"Kind of." I felt heat rising in my cheeks, sensual visions of our kiss painting over my thoughts and sending tingles through my body. "General Rouhr gave Rokul and me an assignment. I need to find him."

"Oh." Takar's expression brightened slightly. He and Rokul really were complete opposites. "He should be in the weight room."

I recalled that I'd disrupted his morning exercises and nodded.

"Where is that?" I asked.

"Down the corridor on the right," Takar nodded.

"Thanks!" I took off again, eager to escape the uncomfortable conversation. I wondered what Takar knew.

I found Rokul lifting weights that weighed as much as I did.

"Hey!" I called to him. He looked over his shoulder at me, smiled, and set his weights aside like they were made of air.

"Good morning, again," he grinned. "I didn't think I'd see you so soon."

"We've got an assignment," I smiled back.

"What is it?"

"How would you like to chase down sentient plants and stick them with darts?" I asked.

"It's like you can see into my mind," Rokul laughed. "Does this have something to do with the neutralizers you're trying to make?"

"Yup," I nodded. "Leena created some for me to test."

"So, there's a chance they won't work at all and I'll have to deal with a sentient plant trying to kill us?" Rokul lifted one brow.

"Exactly!" I beamed.

"Even better!"

ROKUL

I was glad that Tella had requested me to be her 'bodyguard' for this trek into the wilderness. Not only was it something to do, but it was more time with her.

"Just wanted to say again, thank you for requesting me," I said as we headed for the aerial unit. I hated the thing. It was loud and annoying, but it accomplished what we wanted, and that was transportation.

"Why wouldn't I?" she asked.

"Figured you would have gotten tired of me by now, you know, me and my gigantic redness and whatnot," I quipped as I helped her into the transport.

"Eh, the red doesn't bother me. Now, your voice, on the other hand…" she grinned as she left the sentence hanging.

"Understood," I said.

Tella chuckled as she buckled herself in. I made my way around to the pilot's side and hopped in. "So, where to?"

"You know where," she said with a look.

We had decided to return to Rigkon, since we already knew from her previous job with Gille there was a plethora of rogue sentient plants there. The one she'd already killed had been infested with whatever those vines were.

Chances were good we'd find more.

"I know, just making sure you hadn't changed your mind or found somewhere more dangerous for us, is all." Before she could respond, I yanked the transport up into the air and pushed the engines hard as I turned us around.

"Hey, easy there, wild man. If you crash us, we have no job and no fun," she yelled over the engine noise. I just laughed at her.

We flew over the trees for a bit before I dared talk again. "Hey!"

"What?" she yelled back.

"What are we going to call this thing?"

"What, this thing?" she asked, indicating the transport. "I thought you guys already had these named."

I shook my head and smiled. "No, not this. The take-over-other-plants-with-vines thing!" I shouted back to her.

"Oh," she said with a lift of her chin. "I don't know. Did you have any ideas?"

"Not off the top of my head," I answered with a shrug. "Let's talk on the ground."

She nodded. It was hard to yell over the engine all the time. I needed to talk to Fen and the other Urai to see if they knew how to modify these things to make them more powerful and quieter at the same time.

It wasn't long before we were back at Rigkon, and it still made me wonder at how people were willing to live in such a ramshackle place. I understood the desire to start over and either build anew or rebuild, but this looked terrible.

We landed and I helped Tella out. "We should make sure to get a few extra supplies from the market," she said as she hopped down.

"Why? I thought we had everything we need," I answered. I honestly thought we had. I was better armed than last time and I had made sure Tella had a few extra weapons, as well. On top of her knife and the two blasters I had given her, she also had her complement of experimental neutralizers that she and Leena had created. Inside the two packs I had brought were food and drink in case we got caught in the wilderness after dark.

She looked at me as if I was stupid. "We should get some *extra supplies* from these people." She was trying to tell me something, I knew it.

Ah, she had said 'extra' supplies. With a nod, I agreed with her and grabbed the packs from behind her seat. She meant for us to spend a little money in the market of the town, the extra income being something they couldn't count on from one another.

"About time you got it, goof," she said with a smile as she took her pack and started to walk away from me. As I caught up to her, she looked up at me.

"What have your teams been calling the monster plant?" she asked, refreshing the topic of choice on the flight over.

"The target?" I joked, then quickly backed off at her glare. "You're the expert in plant-life," I said. "Anything I come up with would be stupid, as you would most likely point out."

"Eh, probably. But," she stopped at a booth in the market and negotiated with the proprietor for a few extra fruits and some water.

She looked at me and indicated one of the other booths, this one with some interesting looking knives on display. Guess they didn't have the same people at the booths every day. I approached the booth and the vendor took an involuntary step back. I tried to smile reassuringly but that made them step back more.

"Hello," I said politely as I stopped to look at the knives. They looked to be in good condition, nicely serrated on one side, with a sharp edge on the other. "May I?" I asked as I reached for a knife whose blade was as long as my hand.

A nervous nod answered me. I picked up the knife. It had a good weight to it, was well-balanced, and when I tested the edge against my thumbnail, it cut into my nail as if it were water. A few practice swings, after making sure no one was near, solidified my opinion, this was a good knife. "How much?" I asked.

"It, it, it's t-t-t-twenty, sir." The vendor was a medium-built human male, young looking. He must never have seen one of us up close if he was this nervous.

"Did you make this?" I asked, holding the knife by the blade and handing it back to him. "It's nice." The compliment did wonders. His hesitation fairly flew away as he acknowledged that he indeed had made the knife.

"Learned from my daddy, before...you know." I did. I answered him with a nod.

"Tell you what," I started. "I'll buy this one for fifteen, but to make it worth your while, if you can get me," I stopped to think for a moment. Should I get one for just my team, or all three teams? Skrell it. "If you can make me another fifteen of these, I'll take each one of those off your hands. What do you say?"

I didn't think anyone's eyes could get any larger. He nodded, told me it would be maybe two weeks before he was done with them all, and accepted payment. As he handed me my new knife, he thanked me profusely.

"My pleasure..." I hesitated. I had no idea what his name was or who to look for.

"My name is Umi," he said. "I can have the knives ready and waiting for you here in two weeks. Thank you."

"Umi," I repeated his name as I extended my hand. He took it without hesitation. Compliments did wonders for a person's confidence, I thought as we shook hands. "My name is Rokul. Unless I get killed, I'll be back for the knives." I went ahead and paid him half of the price for the fifteen knives, promised him the rest of the payment upon delivery, and turned around to see Tella watching me.

"What?" I asked as I strapped my new knife to my thigh.

"Nothing," she smiled. "So, have you thought of what to call this vine?" As we slowly made our way into the surrounding trees, we batted around ideas...some funny, some serious. Finally, we settled on the human definition of a Skotan word, zerl. A zerl was someone that controlled someone or something else. Tella said that that sounded a lot like a Puppet Master. I liked it. We ran with it.

It wasn't long before we found a kodanos. This one was alone. While, in my experience thus far, kodanos only attacked when threatened, this one immediately began approaching when it saw us.

"I'll distract it, you get behind it," I said to Tella as I started moving to my left. She didn't argue and immediately took a few steps back into the trees and headed to her right, making her way behind the kodanos.

I had to be careful with this thing. The kodanos had its own defenses with its whip-like tendrils, but it also housed some nasty little beasties the locals had dubbed talusians. Talusians were ugly things with wings, three eyes, and teeth sharper than my new knife. I kept yelling at the kodanos in an attempt to keep its attention on me. It whipped one of its tendrils at me, sending me diving to the side to avoid being struck.

I took out one of my knives, not the new one, and held it in front of me as I stayed in a low crouch. As it stepped towards me again, I noticed that it didn't move anything like a normal kodanos. Now, a kodanos didn't have the most graceful gait I had ever seen, but it was certainly more graceful than this bumbling monstrosity.

I could see Tella come out of the trees behind it. It

was time to make sure its full attention was on me. As it whipped a tendril at me again, I took a step back and swung my knife. I felt the knife bite into the tendril and rip a bit as I pulled it back.

The kodanos stepped back, let out a silent howl, and opened itself up. Fully expecting a barrage of talusians to come flying at me, I braced myself, but nothing happened. It was empty.

I didn't have time to think about it as it swung at me again. Meanwhile, Tella had been firing neutralizers into the back of it, all to no avail. Fantastic.

As I swung my knife again, fully expecting a long and painful fight, the kodanos started to secrete some sort of gas. My head started to feel funny as my vision blurred. Everything changed color and began to blend together in a swirling vortex.

The last thing I remembered was dropping my knife and Tella screaming my name.

TELLA

I screamed as Rokul fell to the ground. The kodanos, previously unaware of my position, swung around to face me.

My first instinct was to clamp my lips shut. Screaming was never a good idea in a situation like this. But when the kodanos took a step away from Rokul's body, I realized this situation could be the exception.

"Hey!" I lifted my hands over my head, clapping and waving them to hold the attention of the kodanos. I trilled my tongue as I backed away. With luck, the kodanos would step away from Rokul. Unfortunately, my distraction worked too well. The kodanos let out a roar and burst forward with shocking speed.

Recalling how I took down the other kodanos last time I was in this section of forest, I sprinted toward the nearest tree. I pushed off the ground and reached for the lowest branch, with the intention of pulling myself out of the path of the raging kodanos. Wood splinters pierced my palm as I gripped the branch. I swung my leg to the trunk to use it as leverage. As soon as I put the weight of my foot against the trunk, the bark caved in. The branch I gripped snapped under my weight. This tree was dead.

"Shit!" I scrambled away from the tree as it began to collapse. The trunk fell forward, striking the charging kodanos. As the kodanos thrashed at the dead tree trunk, I got to my feet and ran. I made sure not to move closer to Rokul, but I didn't want him out of my sight, either. My stomach clenched in fear as I imagined a living vine wrapping around Rokul's leg and dragging him off, deep into the wood, for me never to see again.

Something fell out of my jacket pocket. I crushed it beneath the sole of my boot as I ran. It was one of the empty vials that once contained an experimental neutralizer. Something else fell out of my pocket, as well.

It was some kind of miracle that I didn't step on it, too.

It was the dart I'd purchased from the Rigkon market the day I met Rokul.

I doubled back and scooped it up. Thankfully, the chamber containing the thick red toxic liquid was undamaged. The dart was meant to be used with some kind of gun that I didn't possess.

Rokul might've had something in the armory that would've worked, but I'd stupidly forgotten to ask about it.

I'd completely forgotten about the whole thing, to be honest, what with all the chaos of a new plant form, attacks on settlements, and a big red goof that had taken up far too much of my thoughts.

Dodging the kodanos wasn't difficult. The invasive vines of the Puppet Master might've made it quicker and more aggressive, but it still couldn't make tight turns without the risk of toppling over. I wove between the trees, keeping the kodanos on my trail, as I tried to figure out how I was going to inject the toxin.

I moved in a wide circle with Rokul at the center, always in view. When I reached an area opposite to where I'd been hiding earlier, I spotted an overgrown tree trunk almost completely hidden from view. Hoping it wouldn't crumble beneath my feet, I leaped onto it and scrambled to the highest point.

The kodanos lumbered closer. I'd planned to jump onto it and drive the tip of the toxic dart into the thinnest part of its bark exterior at the base of its thick neck. The issue was, the kodanos wouldn't turn its back to me.

It was close enough to strike at me. If I didn't move,

or do something, I'd end up in the same condition as Rokul. A faint hissing sound caught my attention. The air around me smelled...strange. I couldn't place it. Instinctively, I held my breath. The air around the kodanos looked blurry. I realized it was secreting some kind of gas, which wasn't something a normal kodanos was able to do on its own.

I had to move. If the kodanos didn't strike me down, then the gas would. With no other option, I leaped forward at the kodanos. I collided with its chest, slamming the dart into its neck with every ounce of my strength. It closed its massive branch-arms around me. It wasn't able to pry me off its body, so it began to squeeze.

My bones barked in protest. I would've cried out if I'd been capable of making any sound. Certain I was going to die, I opened my eyes and looked at Rokul lying on the forest floor.

I hoped that he would wake up soon and get back to the capital alive.

For a moment all of the possibilities with him, the future I'd been so afraid of, seemed so precious.

And now it would never happen.

The pressure on my body suddenly ceased. The kodanos let out a shuddering rattle. Its legs buckled beneath it and it began to fall forward. Realizing I was about to be crushed, I wriggled out of its loosening grasp and rolled as soon as I hit the floor. I took in a rasping breath then immediately realized my mistake. The gas was still in the air. My head felt like it was filled with the numbing extract of a phythmo plant.

The kodanos fell, motionless against the fallen tree trunk. The vines of the Puppet Master burst through every weak spot in the kodanos's body. They writhed and twisted over each other like they were on fire before shriveling up and turning black.

Well then. Let's have more of that.

Certain that the kodanos and the Puppet Master's vines were dead, all I wanted to do was lie down. The spongy piles of decaying leaves that made up the forest floor looked soft and inviting.

Rokul! A sane voice in my mind snapped, forcing my drooping eyelids to open.

"Rokul," I said out loud, though I couldn't tell if I whispered or shouted his name. On unsteady legs, I stood up and made my way back towards him. I stumbled and tripped over my own feet often, but as I gulped in untainted air, my mind cleared.

Rokul, on the other hand, was still in the grips of the gas. I watched the steady rise and fall of his chest to make sure that he was able to breathe. I carefully checked him over for more serious injuries, any broken bones or lacerations. There were none, other than a few superficial scrapes that had managed to get through his scales. Satisfied that there were no concerning injuries, I smacked his shoulder.

These arms needed to hold me again. He needed to wake up.

"Hey!" I shouted. "Rokul, wake up!" No response. I gave him a firm shake, tapped his cheeks with my fingertips, and even leaned close to whisper in his ear. Nothing worked. A sinking feeling in my heart threatened to overtake me. I wanted to kiss him, close my eyes, and hear the rain again, be in his embrace, safe in bed.

"I guess we'll just have to wait this out." I made an effort to sound cheerful, though I wasn't sure if he could hear me or not. "That's fine. I don't think you get enough sleep, anyway."

Rokul said nothing, not that I was expecting him to talk. I sat in the silence of the forest for a few moments before I stood up again.

"I should at least try to get you back to Rigkon," I reasoned.

I stood by his head and tried to work my hands under his arms. He was heavy, far heavier than any human male could ever be. Muscles and bone density must be higher. For a moment I wondered about the gravity of his homeworld. Something to ask about later. Because dammit, we were having a later.

I tugged at his unconscious body, but it was like

trying to move a boulder. After a few minutes of pulling, yanking, and jerking, I gave up.

I sat down next to his head with a huff.

"How long is this supposed to last, do you think?" I asked him. "How much of that stuff did you inhale? At least I had the good sense to hold my breath." I found myself wishing that Rokul heard everything I said. I could imagine the snark he'd fire back, but it wasn't as satisfying as hearing the words from his mouth.

"Do you think the gas you've inhaled is the same one released during the attacks on the settlements?" I wondered aloud. "It would make sense if it was. Yet, I don't recall unconsciousness being a side effect of that gas, just memory loss. I'll see what you remember when you wake up." I gave Rokul a pat on the arm.

I shifted so my back pressed against the side of his body. In the silence of the forest, I listened for any sign of danger. I clutched the hilt of my hunting knife and watched the light drain out of the forest. I hadn't realized it was so late.

The bioluminescent bacteria colonies began to stir. Though they were fainter than they should've been, their glow was still enchanting to look at. Tiny insects flickered in the smoky blue light of dusk.

"I wish you were awake for this," I said to Rokul. Of course, he didn't reply.

Now that the sun had set, the warmth it left behind

leeched out of the forest. I wrapped my arms around myself, shivering. I was tempted to start a fire, but I didn't want to risk drawing attention to our location and ultimately decided against it.

My teeth chattered as the cold seeped into my bones.

If Rokul was awake, he'd laugh at me and tell me it wasn't cold to begin with. That wouldn't stop him from putting his arms around me to keep me warm.

"You have to wake up at some point, okay?" I said, suddenly feeling afraid. What if the gas sent people into comas? What if he wasn't going to wake up without some kind of antidote? I couldn't lose him like this.

I found myself wishing I'd walked back to Rigkon while it was still light out. Someone there might've been willing to help me bring him back to the guesthouse. Swiggen liked me well enough.

Maybe.

But it was too late to go back to Rigkon now. I couldn't leave Rokul alone in the dark.

Rokul's skin was still warm, which was a good sign, right?

I laid down beside him, wedging myself between his arm and his side. Warm and somewhat comfortable, happy to feel him against me at least, I continued to scan the glowing forest. I didn't feel the least bit tired as I watched the flickering bugs dip and swirl in the air.

With every rustle, my body went rigid and I reached for the hunting knife, but nothing attacked us. Now I felt grateful that Rokul had killed the Helmria Ithalma when we first met. If he hadn't, I bet it would've come after us long ago.

Periodically, I checked to make sure Rokul was still breathing. After a few hours of sitting in the dark, jumping at shadows, I looked at Rokul's face.

"At least one of us is getting a good night's sleep," I laughed.

ROKUL

It was too bright when I woke up the next morning. My entire body ached from head to toe.

What the hell did I do last night?

My thoughts were slow to form and fractured, but I was slowly able to piece together what happened. Tella and I were going to test out the neutralizers she and Leena cooked up in the lab. We returned to Rigkon and found an aggravated kodanos. After that, I didn't remember anything.

When my eyes adjusted to the light, I saw Tella sitting cross-legged on the forest floor with her back to me.

"Tella." My voice was scratchy, like I hadn't used it in a while. Tella whipped around, the sunlight gleaming through her hair.

"You're awake!" she gasped, then twisted around and threw her arms around my neck.

"What happened?" I asked. "Where's the kodanos?"

"Dead over by that fallen tree," she said. "It knocked you out."

A memory flashed in my mind's eye. The kodanos towered over me but, for some reason, I couldn't properly fight back. I recalled feeling suddenly drowsy when it approached me. The air had smelled strange around the kodanos.

"Did it use gas?" I half-guessed.

"Yes," Tella nodded.

"I didn't know they could do that," I said.

"They can't. I think that new feature was courtesy of the Puppet Master." As she spoke, I noticed that she looked paler than usual. There were deep circles under her eyes again. She hadn't looked that tired when we'd arrived in Rigkon.

"How'd you kill it?" I asked.

"I purchased a toxin-filled dart last time I was in Rigkon," she explained. "Honestly, I completely forgot I had it. It killed the kodanos, but unfortunately, it also destroyed the vines."

"I don't have anything to launch a dart." My brow furrowed.

"I jumped on the kodanos and stabbed it in the neck," she explained sheepishly. My eyes went wide.

"I can't believe I missed that!" I exclaimed. "I've been eager to see you in action ever since that disgusting flower got the best of you on the day we met."

"The Helmria Ithalma isn't disgusting," Tella shook her head.

"It eats people." Really, did it need to have anything else before it was firmly in the not-okay-to-keep-as-a-pet column?

Tella released her grip on me and moved back so I could sit up. "How are you feeling?"

"Like I got knocked out by a sentient tree," I laughed. "How long was I out? I hope I haven't kept you waiting too long." Tella bit her lip and looked away. I frowned, looking around. The light was wrong, not what I expected.

"What is it, Tella?"

"You were out a while" she said. "The kodanos knocked you out yesterday."

"We've been out here all night?" I exclaimed. That's why she looked so exhausted. "You didn't sleep at all, did you?"

"I stayed up to make sure nothing came after us in the dark," Tella explained. "It wasn't that bad." Now it was my turn to wrap my arms around her.

"Humans aren't supposed to stay awake for that long," I murmured. "Are you well?"

"I'm a little tired, but it's not that horrible for a

human to stay up all night every once in a while." I felt her smile against the skin of my neck.

"Weren't you cold?" I asked.

"A little. But even unconscious, you're an excellent heater," she laughed.

"We should get you home immediately," I insisted.

"We should stop in the guesthouse first," Tella replied. "You don't seem to have any wounds, but I think you should let me clean you up before we head back."

"Absolutely not," I said firmly. "You've been up all night. You need to sleep."

"Let me check to see if you do have any wounds and I'll take a nap in the guesthouse before we head back," she suggested. "Your scales protected you from a lot of damage, but I couldn't check your back. You're too heavy."

"That's what they're there for," I grumbled as she began to prod my body.

"You still got your ass kicked by a plant," she teased.

"It cheated with knockout gas."

"Sore loser." She rolled so that she was halfway on top of me. I could tell she was holding herself gingerly so avoid putting any of her weight on me. I wrapped an arm around her lower back, bringing her fully down on me.

With her face so close to mine, it was impossible not

to kiss her. Her lips were soft and tasted sweet, like berries.

"Did you have a late-night snack?" I asked her.

"Possibly," she admitted before bringing her mouth back to mine. My arm ached as I lifted my hand to cup the back of her head. With my other arm, I coaxed her over so she was lying completely on top of me.

"I don't want to hurt you," she whispered against my mouth. I laughed against her lips.

"I hate to break it to you, but you're not nearly as big and strong as a kodanos."

As her body relaxed against mine, the sensation behind the kiss shifted into something heady and hungry.

I wrapped my arms tighter around her, holding her against my chest, sliding my hand down to knead the lush curve of her ass.

My mind returned to our first night together, when we stumbled along a barely-there dirt road.

We were strangers, then. And drunk.

And I wanted her even more now.

From the way Tella gently rocked her hips against me, I felt that she agreed.

"I was terrified you weren't going to wake up," she whispered between kisses. "When you spoke to me, I'd never felt so happy in my life."

I slid my hand under her shirt and stroked the soft, bare skin of her back.

"The only thing better than waking up to you watching over me is waking up to you sleeping soundly beside me," I whispered back.

I nudged Tella so that her legs fell on either side of my waist. She rocked her hips again, stoking my arousal.

"If you keep doing that, you'll be in trouble," I growled and nibbled her earlobe.

"Haven't you noticed? I chase trouble," she murmured back.

That was my undoing. I pressed myself against her.

"I want you *now*," I hissed. "All of you."

Never had I had less control than I did in this instant.

"Take me," she ordered.

It seemed she had the same overriding needs that I did.

I wouldn't need to be commanded twice.

She raised herself, and my hands went to the waistband of her pants, shoving them past her knees to reveal her sweet sex to me.

Her hands were quicker and defter than mine. She freed my hardened cock from its constraints. Hands gripping her hips, I dragged her over my length once, twice, watching her eyelids flutter as she ground against every ridge.

I could be drunk on just the feel of her honey against my skin. But I wanted more.

Sliding my arms under her succulent thighs and spreading her wide, I lifted her up, over my face.

"Hold on, beautiful," was the only warning I gave her before I brought my tongue to her folds. My mouth closed over her blooming flower of a perfect pussy and I sucked her clit, licked her lower lips until she screamed my name.

She fell back, and I caught her, one hand supporting her back, feeling every quiver run through her body as I kept licking, nibbling at her until she convulsed again.

I raised her back up until she sat at my waist, then pulled her to my chest, stroking the sensitive skin of her back as her shudders slowed.

Reaching around her thigh, I slid one finger between her folds from behind, piercing her heat, driving into her until she gasped again.

Tella's pliable, melting body in my hands and mouth was perfection.

"Now, baby," I purred, then dragged the head of my weeping cock against her soaked pussy. She moaned, deep and low, as I rocked my hips, working each ridge deeper inside her.

Still so tight, so hot.

"Are you alright?" I managed, even as all I wanted was to bottom out inside her, make her mad with desire as I claimed her.

"God, yes," she murmured, then pushed herself up, knees holding her above me. The sight was too much.

I grabbed her hips, pulling her down further as she cried out, working my way deeper into her.

Tella straightened up and tipped her head back as I impaled her. As I lifted her up and down, I watched the hypnotic sway of her breasts beneath her shirt. With each thrust, my body ached, but nothing outweighed this delicious pleasure.

Nothing ever would.

"Is this how you imagined it when we stumbled out of the Crooked Swiggen?" she panted.

"Oh no," I grinned as I buried myself inside her again. Almost to the hilt now. "I had something else in mind."

"Tell me," she said.

"That would ruin the surprise," I teased. "But be assured that I planned on spending hours bringing you to every imaginable height of pleasure." She let out a shuddering gasp as, with one final thrust, I drove into her, all the way to the hilt.

My hands at her hips kept her still as I pounded up into her, the feel of her heat surrounding me driving me wild, knocking aside any semblance of control I'd ever had.

Isolated in the forest, with the sentient plants driven away by the strange kodanos and no one to hear, Tella didn't muffle her cries of pleasure. Listening to her gasps and feeling her reach that peak drove me over the edge and pushed me into my own climax.

With a floaty sigh, Tella leaned forward and collapsed against my chest. I wrapped my arms around her, holding her to me.

This, right here, right now, was all I'd ever wanted. We could stay like this forever.

Unfortunately, we were still on a mission.

When our breathing slowed, Tella slowly stood up and righted her clothing. I did the same.

"We should get back. I'm sure the others are worried about us." I leaned in and planted a kiss on her forehead. But no sooner did I say that than my mouth slid lower, kissing her long sooty eyelashes before those eyes fluttered at me, and I captured her mouth with mine.

She moaned into my mouth and my willpower was tested then and there.

But she pulled away first. "Let's go report in." Her pink tongue swiped at her lips, and I nearly brought her to the ground, eager to taste her all over again. "And then let's find a real bed, alright?"

TELLA

Rokul and I returned to General Rouhr's building looking like we'd been through hell, but neither of us could stop smiling.

At least that was the case until I brought up the doctor.

"You have to go see the doctor General Rouhr keeps on staff," I insisted as I walked through the front door Rokul held open for me.

"I told you, I'm fine," Rokul repeated. "Do you think I could've taken part in this morning's activities if I wasn't fine?"

"Yes, actually," I laughed.

"Good, because you're right." Rokul threw an arm over my shoulder. "That kodanos could've ripped my arm off and I still would've wanted you."

"Flattery won't distract me from marching you to the doctor's office," I warned him.

"There's no doctor on duty," Rokul said breezily.

I rolled my eyes.

"Yes, there is. Her name is Evie Parr and Leena tells me she's extremely talented when it comes to dealing with reluctant alien babies," I prodded him.

"I was hoping you wouldn't know about her," Rokul muttered.

"Clearly," I chucked. "Now, come on! I'll never sleep again if I don't know for a fact that the gas you inhaled won't cause any lasting damage." I pulled him through the building by the wrist.

"Fine, for your sake, I'll go get checked out," he sighed.

"I'm walking you to the door," I insisted.

"Don't you trust me?" I looked over my shoulder at Rokul. He had the audacity to look pouty.

"Only when my life's at risk," I replied. "I don't trust you to take care of yourself when your life's at risk."

"I am both honored and insulted at the same time," Rokul chuckled.

"I'm starting to understand how your brother feels," I replied.

Rokul and I approached the medical office, which was only a few doors down from the lab. The medical office was empty, which I took as a good sign. However, I didn't see Dr. Parr.

"Hello?" I called.

"Back here!" A light, chipper voice called from out of sight. I moved to the back of the suite and found a petite blonde woman with an easy smile.

"Hi," she said brightly. "Rokul, I never thought I'd see you in here."

"Don't give me the credit. Tella dragged me here very much against my will." Rokul fixed me with a look. I grinned up at him, feeling quite smug.

"Good job," Dr. Parr gave me an approving nod. "He skipped his mandatory examination after the final battle with the Xathi and he's been ducking me ever since."

"Because I'm perfectly fine and I don't need to waste your time," Rokul explained.

"My time is wasted when I don't have someone to help," Dr. Parr smiled. She turned to me. "If you have work to do, you can leave. I'll make sure he doesn't make a break for it." Something in me told me not to doubt Dr. Parr.

"Thank you," I smiled at Dr. Parr. Before I left, I turned to Rokul. "Be good."

"Aren't I always?" He winked and I tried to hide my blush from the doctor as I left the medical office.

When I walked into the lab, Leena was asleep at her

station. I gingerly poked her in the shoulder to wake her. Leena's head shot up and she muttered something incoherent.

"You were asleep," I explained as Leena looked at me in confusion.

"I skipped my morning coffee," she shrugged. "Clearly, that was a bad idea."

"Do you sleep here?" I asked her.

"No," she replied. "Axtin came in early and I decided to go with him. I don't like sitting in my apartment alone."

"I see." Leena blinked a few times before taking in my disheveled state.

"You can't tell me you didn't get laid last night," she smirked.

This time, I didn't try to hide anything. I grinned back.

"Finally!" Leena exclaimed. "But why do you have leaves and crap in your hair?"

"We might've been in the forest," I chuckled.

"You got laid when you were supposed to be field testing my neutralizers?" Leena gasped.

"I tested the neutralizers first! Then I got laid." Leena and I laughed for a moment before forcing us to get down to the serious work.

"How did the neutralizers work?" she asked.

"They didn't," I frowned. "None of them worked in the slightest."

"That's impossible," Leena shook her head. "Every simulation said that those neutralizers would affect the target."

"I thought the simulations were imprecise," I recalled.

"They are, but they all indicated that any of the neutralizers would affect the target in some way," Leena clarified.

"We tested them on an infested kodanos. They don't naturally possess any ability to immobilize toxins in their body," I explained. "They also don't naturally secrete a sleeping gas, but that happened, too."

"Do you think the vines from that creature neutralized the neutralizer?" Leena lifted her brows.

"It must've. A kodanos couldn't have done it on its own," I said. "Rokul and I have started calling the creature the Puppet Master."

"That's fantastic and all," Leena nodded. "A new name doesn't change the problem, though. We're back to square one and General Rouhr's going to pull the plug on this tomorrow."

"Not completely." I pulled the empty dart from my pack. "I bought this at the market in Rigkon the day Rokul was sent to fetch me."

"What was in it?" Leena picked up the dart to examine the empty casing.

"A rare toxin. I've only come across it a handful of times. I don't know how it ended up in Rigkon," I explained.

"What's it made from?" Leena asked.

"Narrisiri extract, according to the shopkeeper" I admitted. "This is the first time I'd purchased it. People have different names for it, too."

"Maybe I can get a profile off of the casting," Leena replied. She took apart the dart and swabbed the inside of the chamber where the toxin was kept. "You used it on the kodanos?"

"Yes," I confirmed. "It killed the kodanos quickly. The vines died shortly after."

"At least it worked on the vines," Leena replied.

"Yes, but I didn't inject the vines directly," I said. "Which may mean the Puppet Master doesn't just physically take hold of its host. It seems to completely integrate itself into its host's nervous and vascular systems, and I wouldn't be surprised if it linked itself to its digestive system, too."

"If you're right, that's going to make it hard to separate the vine from the host without harming the host," Leena replied.

"Maybe you can reduce it the same way you did the pesticides," I suggested.

"It depends on what this is," Leena replied. "I'm running a general test just to get the profile of the toxin." She placed the swap in a shallow dish filled with a gel-like liquid and placed it inside a chamber on one of her lab machines.

"In any other lab, that would take hours," I commented. "How long does it take with alien tech?"

"About thirty seconds," Leena grinned. "I could never work in a human only lab after this. I've been spoiled by innovation."

The machine beeped, indicated the profiling test had been completed. Leena pressed a few buttons and transferred the information to her datapad. When she pulled up in the information, she frowned.

"There's a lot of blank spots," she said. "You were right when you said the toxin's rare. The test didn't pick up on half of its profile. I can run more in-depth tests, but that will take a little longer."

"Let me see." Leena handed the datapad to me and I examined the results of the test.

"Well, it looks plant-based, but with so many missing pieces, it's hard to determine. May I borrow this?" I asked. Leena nodded. I took the datapad to my own station and cross-referenced with a detailed archive of plant profiles. I'd used this archive many times over the years, I'd even added to it myself.

"I've got a partial match," I said.

"You don't sound very excited," Leena observed.

"It's only a forty-three percent match," I frowned. "It's a flower that only grows in the rocky foothills near Glymna. I've worked with that flower before. It doesn't have toxic properties."

"It's a starting point," Leena replied. "I can try to replicate it with known toxins. Maybe it's something as simple as a mix."

"I'm not convinced the toxin in this dart came from that plant at all," I replied. "There are a few key markers missing, markers that would've been identified if they were present in the sample."

"You think it came from a different plant?" Leena asked.

"Possibly," I said. "Or something else entirely. A forty-three percent match isn't as good as it sounds. Fifty-seven percent of the profile comes from something unknown."

"I'll start running the genetic sequence test and the chemical profile," Leena offered. "Hopefully that will give us more information. In the meantime, I can work on recreating the known components of the toxin. It won't kill anything, but it'll be a base to work from. Who knows? Maybe all I have to do is mix it with pesticide and it'll work."

"That would be great," I smiled through a sudden wave of exhaustion. It wasn't just the fact that I didn't sleep last night. "Why can't anything have a simple answer anymore? I feel like every time we make a breakthrough, we're shoved three steps back."

"That's how I felt when I worked through the Xathi invasion," Leena replied. "But we got through that and we'll get through this. The process is going to be a pain in the ass, but we'll get through it."

ROKUL

I wasn't terribly happy with myself. The fact that I had been beaten by a tree rankled me.

Yes, it had done something that the kodanos had never done before, according to Tella, but I had still been beaten by a tree.

A tree!

And then I had to go to the doctor.

I made my way to Rouhr's office for my report. Just as I entered and was about to be greeted by Tobias, the ground began to shake. Tobias let out a small shriek and ducked under his desk while I dropped my report.

The light streaming in through a nearby window was suddenly blocked by something large and green.

I rushed outside to see that a massive vine that was nearly as thick as I was snaked up the side of the building. The further up it got, the thicker it became. As it moved, the building shook and pieces of it crumbled off, forcing me out into the middle of the street in order to avoid being struck.

I looked around the city to see more vines climbing up more buildings. Windows shattered above me, showering me with tiny bits of glass. I shook myself clean and looked towards the lab. There was a vine climbing up it, as well.

TELLA!

I sprinted back towards the building, trying my best to maintain my balance as the ground shook and moved under me. I could hear screams and shouts emanating from the buildings near me, and from nearby parts of the city. There were several people hiding in doorways, their eyes filled with fear as they held on to one another.

A piece of building came crashing down into the street in front of me, dirt and debris pelting me as I hurdled it. A nearby shout caught my attention. A man had been pinned under a corner of a building that had fallen, and three men were around him. With a soft curse, I rushed over.

"What's the matter?" I shouted.

"He's pinned." I took a quick look, found a good place for leverage, and placed my shoulder under a small ledge.

"When I push, you and you," I pointed at two of the men standing there, "help me lift. While we lift, you," I pointed to the last man, "pull him out." At their nods, I took a deep breath and pushed up. The two men helped me lift the piece of building and the other pulled him out.

The man had passed out from pain and blood loss already. His leg looked terrible. "Get him to the infirmary as safely as you can! GO!"

I didn't wait to see if they followed orders. The shaking was getting worse. I stumbled my way to the lab entrance. It was in the same building as Rouhr's office, but the outside entrance was on the other side of the building.

I pushed through the door and raced to Tella's lab. When I broke through the door, she rushed over to me from her hiding place in a doorway. "Rokul!"

"Tella. Are you okay?" I asked over the sound of a few beakers falling to the ground.

She nodded, then jumped as one of the interior windows shattered. "Yeah, for now. What's happening?"

Before I could answer, the shaking became worse. Things fell from the walls, ceiling tiles tumbled to the ground, light bulbs popped, and one of the taller shelves fell over, breaking over the top of a lab table.

"Get under a table!" I shouted. We half dragged, half pushed one another under a nearby lab table as the shaking continued. I watched as a crack formed in a floor tile and drunkenly made its way across the floor, stopping a few inches from my hand.

The shaking went on for what felt like hours, but when all was said and done, it must have lasted only a few minutes. I pulled myself away from Tella's embrace enough to chance a glance from under the table.

The lab was in shambles. Light fixtures hung from the ceiling, floor tiles were cracked or broken, one of the interior windows was shattered while the others were all cracked. The only thing that didn't seem damaged was the table we had ducked under.

Tella looked frightened.

She never looked frightened.

Scro.

I grabbed her and kissed her hard, willing all of my comfort to her. All of my—

Then I regretfully broke it off. "We have to see how much damage the vines caused."

Surprise registered not only on her face, but in her voice. "This wasn't just an earthquake?"

I shook my head. "Uh-uh." I had apparently picked up some of the human ways of answering. "This was done by vines. Let's go." I crawled from under the table and helped her to her feet. We slowly and carefully made our way outside.

Of all the things that I could have possibly imagined

when I stepped outside the door, what I did see would never have entered my mind unless I had seen it. It had been a bright morning, the sun almost blinding in the clear sky. Now, sunshine came through in scattered lines, barely illuminating the city. We were inside of a dome.

The vines that had come out of the ground stretched high into the air, several hundred feet. The vine that had crawled its way up the general's building went straight up, and up, and up until it connected with more vines.

It acted as a pillar for the vine-dome that covered us. As we looked around, I noticed nearly a dozen other such 'pillars' stretching high into the sky.

I pulled Tella around to the front of the building, and came face-to-face, so to speak, with just how truly massive this vine-pillar was. It had displaced almost the entire street in front of the office building, stretching an easy twenty feet across. I touched the vine as we made our way around it. It was rough, rubbery, and warm. I could feel the life pulsating through it.

As we rounded the corner, Rouhr, Tobias, and everyone else from the building were coming out, stepping over what was left of the piece of roof that had fallen.

"General," I called out and rushed over, Tella half a step behind me. "Are you alright, sir?"

He nodded. He looked fine, just covered in dust. "No injuries. A small bump to my ribs is all. What is all this?"

"I have no idea sir. But that vine there," I said, pointing to the one that had broken our building. "Is easily twenty feet around. It's..." I was interrupted by one of the women yelling and a few of the men shouting as they pointed upwards.

I turned to look. Hundreds of tendrils the size of my arm began 'falling' from above and sprouting out of the pillars. I grabbed Tella and pulled her behind me. Instinctively, I took a knife from my waist and handed it to Rouhr, and watched Tella pull out her own knife. I grabbed the knife I had gotten from Umi and we all prepared for a fight.

Nothing happened. The tendrils stopped well out of our reach and just moved around of their own volition. There was no pattern, no coherent reason to their movements that I could see.

I let out a string of curses that would have seriously angered my brother, embarrassed my mother, and would have made my father look at me as if I had brain damage.

"Well, that's disconcerting," Rouhr said through a forced chuckle.

I had to agree. Of course, I wasn't sure if he was

speaking about my cursing or the vines, so I assumed the vines. "What do we do now?" I asked.

"We figure out who's hurt, what's broken, and then what all of this is," he answered.

I looked around. It was going to take time to get all of that information. "Well, at least we still have..." before I could finish my statement, several streetlights began popping and the collective hum of city power went silent.

Tella looked up at me, a hand on her hip. "You were about to say that we still had power, weren't you?"

"No," I drew out my answer slowly. "I was going to say, 'at least we still have each other,'" I finished.

"Yeah, sure you were," she nodded knowingly. "You just had to say it, didn't you?"

"What? I didn't even get to finish saying it, so it's not my fault."

"Excuse me?" We both turned back to see Rouhr looking at us, a resigned look clear on his face. "Are we really thinking that jokes are good right now?"

"Sorry," we both said simultaneously. I nodded an apology to Rouhr. "I'll go find the team and see if we can see how bad this all is."

"Thank you." He headed back into the building, which, when I looked at it more closely, it wasn't in bad shape, considering. The windows were broken, or cracked, and a small section of the roof had fallen, but otherwise it still seemed structurally sound.

A quick look around showed that the damage in the surrounding buildings was similar…nothing had been knocked down, just damaged. The hope was that the rest of the city was the same.

"You up for some walking?" I asked Tella.

She shook her head. "I need to get back to the lab, make sure everyone is okay in there and see if the samples are doing anything."

"Okay. See you later?" I asked.

"Of course."

TELLA

The vines had knocked the power out, which meant the lab was nothing more than a room filled with shiny metal boxes until it came back on.

Leena was, understandably, unhappy about that. She hadn't finished running the more complex tests on the contents of the toxin.

I looked out the window at the wall of vines, eager to get outside and collect samples. I didn't need the lab to tell me the vines belonged to the Puppet Master. They couldn't be anything else.

"General Rouhr wants everyone in the conference room," Rokul said to me. He briefly left my side to help clear the corridor to the med bay. As far as I knew, no one within the building had been seriously injured. I expected the med bay would be opened to the public.

"All right," I replied. Before I let Rokul lead me to the conference room, I walked to the nearest window and looked out onto the city. The glass was cracked, but remained in place, unlike most of the other windows in the city. Yet, aside from the windows, there wasn't much damage. It puzzled me.

As Rokul lead me by the hand through the corridor, debris littered the floor. A waterline had burst somewhere. A puddle was rapidly forming on the floor.

"We're going to have our work cut out for us," Rokul sighed heavily.

"After the meeting, will you come with me to collect samples from the vines?" I asked.

"Of course," Rokul agreed. "I'm sure General Rouhr will want us to do a thorough examination of the perimeter. When we were out there just now, we focused on the civilians."

"You didn't notice anything about the vines?" I asked.

"Other than the fact that they're big, green, and very much in the way, no, I didn't," Rokul grinned.

I laughed despite everything. I suddenly felt overwhelmed with gratitude towards Rokul. I appreciated that he could make me laugh even when things were looking grim.

"The general's probably going to want you to take over during the meeting," Rokul continued. "Any idea what you're going to say to everyone? You're the resident plant lady. They're going to look at you for answers."

"They'll be disappointed," I said. "I have no idea what's going on."

"None?"

"Well, I have a theory but I don't have any proof," I replied.

"Care to share?" Rokul asked.

"Sorry, you'll have to wait to hear it with everyone else," I teased. Truthfully, I didn't even have a full theory at the moment. I was counting on the moments between now and General Rouhr calling me up to complete it.

Rokul and I were some of the last to arrive to the conference room.

I spotted Leena right away. She perched in the lap of a massive Valorni I could only assume was Axtin. He had one arm around her waist, holding her to him. She lazily ran her fingers along his arm. It was odd seeing Leena acting affectionate, but not in a bad way. In fact, seeing them together made me think of my time with Rokul. I reached for his hand and squeezed it, letting him feel my affection, too. He squeezed in return and I felt a warm feeling inside that told me that despite anything else, I had something special with Rokul.

General Rouhr began to speak shortly after Rokul and I found a place to stand.

"Naturally, we're all quite shocked by the turn of events," he began. "As of this moment, it does not look as though it's possible to leave Nyheim. However, we will be thoroughly inspecting the base of these vines for a way out. If we are to find one, we'll need to stage another meeting to determine the best course of action. Right now, our efforts should go to tending to the injured and repairing the city. Comm systems are currently down, but we should be able to piggyback a signal to re-establish them on reserve power soon. Once we do, we'll contact Fen to see if she can open a rift."

"Damages are minimal based on initial sweeps," Karzin jumped in.

"How is this even possible?" Sk'lar asked. "In all my years, I've never seen anything like it."

"As our resident plant expert, do you have any thoughts?" General Rouhr asked me.

My tentative theory was still rough around the edges, but it would have to do for now.

"During my last field expedition, Rokul and I came across a kodanos under the influence of the Puppet Master's vines. We tested the neutralizers created by Leena, but they were ineffective. What's concerning about that, besides the obvious, was that it led me to believe the Puppet Master is able to negate most of our pesticides," I explained.

"We're all but defenseless against it, then?" Leena's mate, Axtin asked.

"Not completely," I replied. "I had on my person a rare toxin that was able to kill the kodanos as well as the vines that piloted it."

"We were working on replicating the toxin when we lost power," Leena chimed in. "Until we have power again, there's not much I can do."

"What's the origin of the toxin?" General Rouhr asked.

"Analysis in the lab tells me it's most similar to a rare plant that grows near Glymna," I explained. "However, I don't believe the toxin comes from that plant. While there were some commonalities, there were almost as many differences."

"Like a related plant?" General Rouhr asked.

"Possibly. Possibly something else entirely. Leena and I won't know for sure until the lab is up and running once more. And even then, it doesn't look like we'll be able to stroll out and collect what we need." I laughed dryly.

"Can't we just cut the rekking vines down?" Karzin grumbled.

"What happens to the vines when we slice them down? What's to stop them from toppling into the city and actually destroying buildings," Rokul spoke up. I shot him a thankful smile. He winked in return, a gesture I felt sure didn't go unnoticed by the others in the room.

"Why did it grow in such a particular pattern?" Tu'ver, a K'ver from Strike Team One I knew only through reputation, asked.

"I have some thoughts on that," I said. "When the group of sorvuc attacked the outpost, reports tell me that it took a considerable amount of coaxing to get the sorvuc to attack Strike Team Two, correct?"

"The sorvuc were more interested in destroying the man-made structures rather than the people living there," Rokul confirmed.

"Now that we know those sorvuc were being controlled by the Puppet Master, I believe these vines are a similar principle but on a larger scale and without a host," I explained. I was met with a sea of confused faces. "Unless something happened that I'm not aware of, the last interaction anyone had with the Puppet Master was me when I injected the kodanos host with that toxin."

When no one contradicted me, I moved on.

"This is only a theory, I can't prove it. But if the Puppet Master can neutralize most toxins, it must've been very surprised to come across me with my toxic dart. I believe that it utilized its seemingly limitless web of consciousness to track my movements back to the city. It may have guessed that Nyheim was the source of the toxin and took steps to contain the threat," I finished.

"If that's true, and the Puppet Master views this place as a threat, why didn't it just destroy the city?" Karzin asked.

"That same question could be asked about the earlier attacks on human settlements," General Rouhr jumped in. "If you remember, most of the damage was to physical structures. The lives lost and injuries caused were collateral damage."

"I don't think the Puppet Master's goal is to take lives. If it was, we'd all be dead under piles of rubble right now," I added.

"Goals?" Takar said. "With all due respect, this is a plant we're talking about. It's nothing more than an overgrown weed."

"If you want my opinion, the Puppet Master is showing intelligence so advanced that I don't think we can classify it as a plant anymore." I shrugged. "It's a sentient creature capable of complex planning. We should start thinking of it as an opponent rather than an overgrown weed."

Takar didn't say anything in response. Instead, he

stared me down as he considered my words. When he nodded his head, accepting my opinion, I felt like I'd won some kind of battle. I glanced at Rokul. He grinned with approval.

"What's our next step, then?" Karzin asked.

"Our priority has to be getting through those vines," General Rouhr replied. "I'd like Tella and Leena to do everything they can to recreate that toxin."

"As soon as we have power, we can do that." Leena nodded.

"What about Jeneva?" Axtin asked. "Will the power outage affect her care?"

"Power should be back on by tomorrow," General Rouhr replied. "Once we're finished here, I'll apply to receive one of the city's emergency generators."

"Isn't the woman who delegates that your mate?" Axtin asked with a laugh.

"Yes," General Rouhr chuckled fondly. "But that doesn't mean I get to take shortcuts. I have to prove that our building is important enough to merit one of the limited number of generators. I expect that we'll receive one, I just have to go through the process in the name of fairness."

"What are our orders until then?" Sk'lar asked.

"Get out into the streets. Help where you can," General Rouhr ordered. "The humans are going to look to us to solve this. If they ask, assure them we're doing everything we can. Remind them that this is nothing like the Xathi invasion. Direct them to Dr. Parr if they're injured. Dismissed."

ROKUL

While some reports had been coming in, Rouhr wanted a first-hand account from his own people of what kind of damage had been done to the city. While Vrehx's team went to check the north side of town, Sk'lar's team went east and we went south.

Coming along with the five of us in Team Two were a few of the medics, in case we found more injured, and Tella. This was going to be my first real look at the damage the vines had caused when they shot out of the ground and formed the dome.

The city itself was in the dark. Many of the buildings had no power, and most of the generators that were worth anything had been taken to the medical center, the lab, and a few stores to help keep food preserved. None of the lights worked, and the holes in the dome only let in small shafts of light.

As we made our way to the outskirts of the city, we could see dozens of small head lamps, flashlights, and even small lanterns moving about the streets. The only lights in buildings were candles or, for the few people that had chosen them, fireplaces.

It all added up to create an eerie environment throughout.

What changed it from eerie to frightening for most of Nyheim's denizens were the thousands of tendrils that hung down from the vines. They were everywhere and, on occasion, several would come down and invade homes, stores, and anything they could get into. They poked around, as if they were looking for something, then pulled back up so another section of tendrils could drop down.

A faint scream reached my ears. Off to my left, a section of tendrils dropped down and forced their way into a house.

We were close to the edge of the dome, and the houses and buildings here were hit harder than the buildings where the pillars stood. The massive green vines had pushed up through the ground, breaking through pavement, walls, and streets as if they were paper. Occasionally, a pipe could be seen sticking out of the ground, water or steam emanating from it. A small pipe with electrical wiring had been pushed out of the ground a few feet from a house, but the wires were dead.

The houses in the area had been made of wood and a brownish-red brick, and while most were still standing, a few hadn't been so lucky. Two houses on a street corner had been obliterated, their remnants scattered all over the streets and in neighbors' yards. I had heard that the people inside had suffered some of the worst injuries of all those who'd been hurt.

Tella walked next to me as we brought up the rear. Slung across her left shoulder was a small pack filled with portable equipment that she intended to use to study the vines, if there was a chance to study them. "How are you holding up?" I asked as I stepped over a small piece of rubble that was still in the street.

She looked up at me and forced a smile. "I'm doing alright, considering. How are you doing?"

I shrugged in an attempt to show my nonchalance, "I'm good, better off than these people." I indicated the broken house, and the house next to it. That one no longer had a roof, and the southeast corner of the house was missing, replaced by a vine thicker than me. I followed the vine upwards, the latticework pattern causing me to lose track of the individual vine.

"Yeah. Hope they're doing okay." she said quietly. I looked at her and could see pain and anger in her eyes. A small shudder shook her body as we continued our way around. So far, there were no holes in the dome except towards the top.

"Eyes up, people!" Karzin yelled from up front. I looked up quickly, to see a batch of maybe three dozen, it was hard to count with them wiggling around so much, tendrils as they came down and invade two houses just ahead of us. A few screams travelled to our ears and my hand clenched.

"Sir?"

"No, Rokul," he answered with a slow shake of his head. "We have no idea the repercussions of cutting any of the tendrils. As of right now, they're not harming anyone, just scaring them." His expression made it clear to me he didn't like it either. "The best we can do is wait a few moments, then check on the families. The tendrils will be done soon enough."

He was right. Within a minute, the tendrils pulled up and another set came down in the distance. Karzin motioned to the medics and they ran to check on the families. "Let's keep looking around, inventorying the damage, and looking for anything that might suggest either a weak spot or at least a spot that Tella can study," he ordered.

Tella and I headed for the house with the corner

missing. She wanted to see if there had been any damage done to the vine by the building, hoping there might be a way to get the toxin into the creature's bloodstream.

We looked and, as expected, found nothing. The floor of the house had been pushed up and broken, as had the ground around the base of the vine. There were no scratches, no cuts, not even a pore evident on the vine for Tella to look at. It was identical in all but size to the vine that had damaged the office building.

We left the house and I was surprised to see Tella wringing her hands.

I looked closely at her and could see that she was doing her best to try to hide her panic. At first, I was confused, but then my brain caught up and I realized what her problem was.

The city was locked up, and so was she.

She was independent and loved to move around. She hated to be locked away somewhere, forced to stay in one place for long. She had told me as much shortly after we first met. I reached out and took her hand, giving it a light squeeze as reassurance.

She smiled up at me and squeezed my hand in return. "This is…" she stopped.

"What?" I asked. Karzin and the others were returning from their quick inspections.

"This looks deliberate to me," she finally said.

Karzin nodded in agreement. "I agree. It's almost as if the damage was more of an accident than anything else."

"How so?" my brother asked. I was shocked. It wasn't often that I had something figured out before he did.

"Look around, Takar," I said. "The vines are on the edge of the city, or at least as close as they can be, and the only deaths we've had reported are from debris falling on people, and one unfortunate person that had grabbed hold, then fell."

"Rokul's right," Tella said. "Combine that with the fact that the tendrils," she pointed to another group of tendrils as they came down to search around in the house she and I had just been in, "don't seem to be trying to hurt anyone, either. It's as if they're looking for something."

"But what?" he asked. I had the same question.

"I don't know," she said sadly. "I don't have the answer to that one."

Karzin clapped his hands together, then cringed slightly as it sounded almost too loud for the moment. "Let's keep moving. We have more to investigate. Keep vigilant, just in case the tendrils do become a threat."

We began to make our way east to meet with Team Three, and I took Tella's hand again.

She leaned into me for a moment before straightening back up.

"You're going to be okay," I said after a few yards.

She looked up at me, confusion written all over her face. I resisted smiling. "What do you mean?" she asked.

"I mean, yeah, we're in a dome made from a plant, but we'll find a way out and you'll be okay," I responded.

She scoffed. "How are we supposed to get out of this?" She waved her hand around, indicating the dome. I looked up at it again. It had to stretch hundreds, if not thousands, of feet into the air in order to encompass the entire city, or, at least, the livable part of the city.

"You just figure out a way to make that toxin, we'll figure out a way to cut the vines so we can stick it in."

As soon as Tella and the ladies managed to make more of the toxin, Rouhr would have us find a way to cut the vines deep enough to get the toxin in and let it be of use.

"It's not that easy," she said.

"Sure, it is. We'll get out of here, I know we will." I stopped walking for a moment, which caused her to stop, as well. "Look, the way I see it is, you make the toxin, we inject the toxin, the vines retreat back into their holes, and you're not stuck here anymore. You'll be able to get out there again," I finished with a jerk of my head to indicate the area outside the dome.

"What if it's not that simple?" she asked, voice so soft I almost didn't catch it.

I shrugged. "We'll figure it out. You're too smart and I'm too stubborn to give up."

Karzin called back to us to catch up.

TELLA

By the time it became too dark to work, I was more exhausted than I ever thought I could be.

After General Rouhr ended his meeting, Rokul and I, along with everyone else, ventured outside to help anyone who needed it. Most people were in a state of shock. But injuries were not as common as we'd expected, which only bolstered my theory that the Puppet Master wasn't out to hurt us.

I knew I couldn't have predicted this, but I felt responsible. If my theory was correct, that the Puppet Master had only contained Nyheim in such a way because it knew I possessed something that could kill it, then this was my fault.

I tried not to think about it. I certainly didn't vocalize my thoughts.

Rokul knew something was amiss with me. Every so often, he reached out to give me a reassuring touch on the back or a kiss on the forehead.

Eventually, our work took us in separate directions. He went with his strike team to assess the perimeter. Leena, Annie, and I, along with a few other scientists from Dr. Hines's lab, began to examine the vines. I took enough samples to last me a lifetime.

We also measured the vines as best we could. Some were much thicker than others. They varied in their coloration, though not by much. We still cataloged everything. One small, seemingly insignificant difference could mean the answer to our escape.

Hours passed before I saw Rokul again. He was waiting for me outside the lab after I dropped off my grand collection of samples.

"You didn't have to wait for me," I grinned.

"I've only been waiting a short while," he replied. "Besides, I want to see you home."

"If it's still standing," I joked. "One swift wind could've taken the walls down. Imagine what all that shaking and rattling did to my place."

"I'm sure it's fine," Rokul assured me. "I'm still walking you home, though."

"Thank you." I smiled up at him and laced my fingers through his. We were silent for most of the walk back to my place.

The long day caught up to us, not to mention the long day before that and the long day before that. In fact, the last time I'd truly slept was when Rokul had stayed over in my bed.

That couldn't be healthy.

My rented room was close to the outskirts of the city. As we drew closer to the towering wall of vines, I started to grow nervous. The nerves only worsened when the Blooming Bud came into view and I could see one of the thicker vines pressed up against the building.

"That can't be good," I muttered.

Rokul and I approached the building. Sure enough, the back wall of my rented room had been completely blown out by the vine.

"Let's see if I can get any of my things," I sighed.

"Where will you stay?" Rokul asked.

"Leena sleeps in the lab all the time. I'm sure it'll work for me," I replied.

"Nonsense. You're staying with me. Don't try to argue, I won't hear it." Rokul silenced me before I could say anything.

"Well, how can I refuse?" I laughed. "Thank you. I'd like to stay with you very much."

The inside of my rented room was more or less intact, aside from the single wall that was entirely replaced by the vine.

I packed a small bag of clothing to take to Rokul's

place. All of my important work equipment was already at the lab in General Rouhr's building.

"I hope the owner realizes I won't be paying for this," I joked lamely.

With my bag slung over my shoulder, I let Rokul lead me out of the room. He didn't release my hand until we reached his place halfway across town.

"Takar is either asleep or still at work," Rokul stated.

"Will he mind my being here?" I asked.

"No," Rokul grinned. "He actually quite likes you."

"How can you tell?" I wondered.

"Didn't you see his obvious display of affection?" Rokul asked.

"You mean that little nod during the meeting earlier?" I asked.

"Exactly. That's just about the grandest gesture he's ever made," Rokul laughed.

"I'm…honored?" I said hesitantly.

"You should be," Rokul teased. He led me through the building, up a set of stairs so narrow he had to turn sideways to use them, and through a small door. The entry room was simple, like I expected. There was some semblance of a kitchen on the far side of the room. Rokul led me through the door on the right, into his room, which was simple, as well.

"Not much for decorating?" I joked. Rokul took my bag from me and set it down beside a chest of drawers.

"My room looks much nicer than yours did," he teased.

"I know," I laughed. "I'm grateful to stay here."

"Truthfully, I only offered because I wanted to make sure I had you to myself for a little bit every day." Rokul wrapped his arms around me and pulled me in close. I laid my head on his chest, content to let him support me.

"I think that's a great idea," I replied. "At work you need to battle Leena for my attention."

"And she's always going to win that battle. That woman is terrifying," Rokul laughed.

"Don't worry, I'll protect you," I joked. "I'm glad to have you all to myself in the evenings."

"You can stay here as long as you like," Rokul replied. "But you aren't stuck here. I want to make that clear."

"I'd rather be stuck with you than anywhere else," I smiled up at him.

"Even tangling with a Helmria Ithalma?" Rokul asked.

"Yes," I laughed.

"I must be special, then." Rokul dipped his head and brought his lips to mine.

"You're more than special," I said when we broke apart. "I'm in love with you." I hadn't planned on saying it, though I'd certainly felt it for a while now.

"I'm in love with you, too," Rokul murmured. "I've been wanting to tell you for some time now, but I didn't want to scare you away."

"So, you waited until I was trapped in a plant prison?"

"Yes, the Puppet Master and I worked very hard on this little stunt," Rokul joked.

"You won't scare me off." I rose up to wrap my arms around his neck. "After all, I've tangled with things far scarier than you." I pressed my lips against his. He enveloped me in a deep kiss, wrapping his arms around me and lifting me off my feet.

Giggling against his lips, I wrapped my legs around his waist. He backed up until his legs hit the bed. Without breaking the kiss, he held me to him and fell back onto the bed. Once on top of him, I moved my legs so they were on either side of him, like I did in the forest. His hands traveled over my legs, up my back, and down my arms.

Slowly, he removed my top and then tackled his own. I took a moment to marvel at the brilliant crimson shade of his skin. If I pressed hard enough on his arms, I could feel the solid edges of the concealed scales.

Once I finished gazing at him, Rokul flipped me over so that I was on my back. With one swift movement, he pulled my fitted pants off, as well as my undergarments. I lay naked beneath him, relying on his heat to stay warm. He removed the rest of his clothing and hovered over me.

"Now I can take you the way I've wanted to since the moment I met you," Rokul smiled mischievously as he nudged my legs apart with his knee, then pressed his palm against my pussy. The claiming way he touched me caught my breath in my throat.

"I should've known you were thinking naughty things this whole time," I playfully scolded him.

"It's impossible not to." Rokul brought his lips to mine as his fingers slowly entered me. I arched up into him, a soft moan escaping my lips. This time was different than our tryst in the forest.

That was hot, explosive, and a product of pure passion.

This was different. I felt like I was a smoldering ember and Rokul was the showering of sparks that kept me alight.

This time, it was about love.

Filthy, delicious love. "Tella," Rokul whispered to me in a deeply sensual voice, "get on all fours, my beautiful woman."

I was exhilarated at whatever was about to come and did as he asked, a little unsure of what was going to happen, but knowing I was going to enjoy it immensely.

I felt Rokul's knees spread mine apart and I yelped.

"You look perfect like this," Rokul growled. I could feel the heat of his breath against my pussy.

Then I felt his tongue. Slowly, searingly, it circled around the inside of my thighs. He nestled his nose over my clit and nudged me, nibbled my thighs.

And then he pulled his face away, only to bring it back and capture my clit with his mouth. He sucked and lightly pulled, enough that, without Rokul's firm hands holding me up, I would have fallen over from the sheer strength of the pleasure that surged through me.

"Yes!" I cried out.

Just as I was about to orgasm, though…

He. Stopped.

"Rokul!" I whimpered, my voice desperate.

With a wicked chuckle, he turned me over, cradling my face. Rokul pressed the massive head of his bumpy and scaly cock at my pussy.

Our eyes locked, and my orgasm was a slow-building wave that flooded through me, desire overtaking me. I was in sheer ecstasy. Only he and I existed in these moments.

He thrust into me slowly. I savored every inch of him, shuddering in pleasure each time he filled me. In this moment, nothing existed beyond these four walls. There was no Puppet Master, no prison of vines, and no need to keep moving.

His hips rocked, hard and forcefully, pressing Rokul so deep inside me that I know he touched places that were only marked and claimed by and for him. I yearned for him to take me, to fill me up as only he could with such raw power and emotion that it made me feel like it was almost a transcendent experience to have him inside me.

My hands laced behind his back and gripped him as tightly as I could. My eyes rolled back in their sockets and I spread my knees as wide as I could, pressing my feet against the mattress to roll my hips up to meet him. Then I clenched my inner walls tight around him, strangling his cock with my pussy to pump every ridged inch of him inside me, milking him for all the pleasure either of us could handle.

When I reached another climax, I felt an explosion throughout my body. It wasn't an explosion of fire like it had been in the forest. This was softer and intense enough to leave me trembling even after Rokul reached his peak. Every inch of my skin was desperately sensitive. The slightest brush of his skin against mine was enough to send me into pleasurable shudders all over again.

Rokul rolled off me, and even though he was right beside me, I immediately missed the intimate contact. He pulled back his covers and threw the blankets over our bodies. I curled close to him, wanting as much of my skin to touch his as possible.

My body felt warm, satisfied, and thoroughly spent.

Tucked under Rokul's arm, I finally let my exhaustion take me. I fell asleep knowing that for once, I was exactly where I was supposed to be.

ROKUL

It had been four days since the dome had been created. A grand total of eight deaths throughout the entire city had been reported, six due to damage caused by the formation of the dome, one from a heart attack, and the last due to the power going out. It had resulted in the poor man's ventilator stopping and he ended up suffocating without it. His body had been found by Team One during our first trek out to investigate.

While Takar and I were out investigating the tendrils and vines again, a call came over our comm system. "Whoa, they work?" I asked.

With a perplexed nod, Takar answered his comm. "This is Takar. Yes, sir. Understood, sir. We will arrive as soon as we are able, sir." He clicked off the comm and focused on me. "The general has reestablished communications with the outside, albeit not particularly reliable. He has called all of us back to the office."

"Okay. Let's go." As we started jogging back, I looked over at my brother. "Did he say anything else?"

"Negative. The connection was not as strong as we are accustomed to," he answered as we rounded a corner. "However, he did stipulate that he wants us there quickly. Would you care to pick up the pace?" He grinned slightly as he started jogging faster, forcing me to keep up or fall behind.

"Basically, you want to race, don't you?" I smiled. His answer was to accelerate, just a step before I did. We sprinted back to the office, dodging civilians and hurdling pets along the way. The only reason he won was because a group of tendrils came down and threw me off my rhythm.

"You always have been a sore loser," he commented when I mentioned the tendrils.

"Oh, whatever," I said as we entered the building. "You know I'm faster than you. Hi, Tobias," I said with a nod to Rouhr's assistant.

Tobias smiled in return. "General Rouhr is not in his office, it is still under repairs," he added at my arched eyebrow. "He has taken to using conference room three until the repairs are complete. That way," Tobias pointed to our left, his right and we made the turn. We walked into the conference room to see that Team Three was already there. The rest of our team joined us within a few minutes.

"Any idea what's going on?" I asked. Rouhr wasn't in the room yet.

A collective shake of their heads answered my question. Sylor spoke up as he shifted in his chair. "All I know is that the comms are back in business, mostly, and that gives me hope that the general has been able to contact the outside."

"That's right, I have."

We all turned to see Rouhr enter the conference room from a side door, Tella right behind him. She flashed me a smile and for a moment, all I could think about was how we were making *very good* use of our sleeping arrangements back at the apartment.

As he directed Tella to a seat, Rouhr looked at all of us. "I've managed to get into contact with the ground crews outside the dome. I also have Fen joining via my comm unit."

We watched as Rouhr put his comm down and Fen's voice greeted us.

"What have the ground units said?" Sk'lar interrupted.

With a deep breath, Rouhr started his answer. "They

can't get in, just like we can't get out. I have them working on their own ideas on what can be done from their side." He held up a hand to stop any further comments or questions. "If you would allow me to finish saying what I need to say, perhaps I'll be able to answer your questions before they are asked. Now, as I was saying," he said as he started pacing across the front of the room. "On the bright side of things, attacks around the continent have stopped."

"Which means that I was right," Tella interjected. "The Puppet Master is sentient, and far more intelligent than we had given it credit for."

Rouhr nodded. "Exactly right. Whatever it wants, it believes that it is here. The attacks everywhere else, while I don't presume to understand or know what they were about, I must assume were intended to find something. I could very well be wrong, and it won't be the first time, nor will it be the last, but..." he leaned forward, arms braced against the table as he spoke, "based on my conversations with Tella, and from my own deductions during the past hour, the previous attacks had to be about something specific. It's the only thing that makes sense to me."

I held my tongue. It seemed a more prudent choice to hear what everyone was saying. Perhaps Tella was rubbing off on me.

"Why don't we just have Fen's A.I. create a rift then?" Sk'lar asked.

"I've been in contact with General Rouhr about just that," Fen's voice cut through the conversation in the room. "And I believe there are two main things that will prevent this. The first is that, from our readings, the entire city appears to now be one living organism. We believe this is because the vines have encased the city."

There was silence in the room. Finally, I spoke up.

"Creating the rift while blind to where living beings are would mean that the chance to catch someone in a rift as it forms goes up dramatically," I said soberly.

"That is correct, Rokul," Fen said through the comm unit. "Without knowing exactly where the rift should form, we cannot create one without placing living beings in danger."

"What was the second reason?" I asked.

There was a pause before Fen continued.

"Even if we were to be able to pinpoint a specific area to form a rift, our readings indicate that the gravitational constant is in flux in and around the city," Fen replied.

"How is that even possible?" Axtin asked. "You'd need something massive…"

"Something that's tied into the planet and can control planetary forces like gravitational pull could very well cause circumstances that make it unstable for us to create a rift. Remember that a rift requires a fairly controlled environment. Stability is key. When the gravitational forces fluctuate even slightly, it becomes impossible to maintain a stable rift," Fen concluded.

I looked to Tella as I spoke, "That would mean this Puppet Master is so enormous it's intricately woven into the very core of the planet itself."

She nodded and looked at Rouhr.

He looked around the room and I finally noticed how tired he looked. He must not have been sleeping as he tried to figure all this out. He went on. "While the attacks have stopped, due to the dome closing us from the rest of the crews and the world, resources are highly limited. We're going to need an updated inventory of what we have here. I already have the outside crews making an inventory list of their own."

He sat down, looking defeated for a breath, then drew himself up straight. "We need ideas of our own. I want each of you coming up with ideas on what we can do. Now, I'll turn it over to Tella to give us her thoughts."

Tella nodded a thank you to Rouhr, then leaned forward in her chair. "Well, like the general was saying, we've made contact with the outside world. I'm not sure how the signal is getting through, but I will assume that somehow we're bouncing a signal through a satellite of some sort and it's getting through one of the holes at the top. As for the vines, from what we've been told, they look different on the outside of the dome than inside."

"Why would they look different?" I asked.

"The only thing that I can think of is that because of the tendrils being inside, and the dome having to be here on a long-term basis, the outside of the vines would most likely have some sort of protective surface in order to keep it from burning in the sun, especially at the top," she answered.

"So, if this thing is sentient, like you say," Karzin cut in, "then what is it looking for? If the general is correct, and it *is* looking for something, what could it be?"

"I'm not sure," Tella answered back. "If it's looking for the toxin I used on it back at Rigkon, there's barely any left and I think the tendrils have already searched the lab. My concern, honestly, is why hasn't it simply destroyed the city?"

"Why would it destroy the city?" Takar asked.

"Well," she said as she stood, "like I said, I firmly believe that this creature is sentient, and I think that it somehow thought of the city as a threat. Now that the city is encompassed in this tremendous-sized cage, it hasn't attacked anything else. That means it feels that it has contained the threat and no longer needs to do anything."

"So, you're saying that it's not looking for something, it's containing something?" Sk'lar asked.

"I don't know," she replied.

"Well, what *do* you know, then?"

She shot Sk'lar a look that had two of his own team looking away. I didn't bother to hide my smile of pride. "More than you, and if you'd shut up long enough to let me finish, I can catch you up. M'kay?" She looked away from Sk'lar and patently ignored his glare. I loved her so much at that moment. "Now, I was going to say that, I don't know if it's simply trying to contain us, but I'm certain that it's looking for something."

"How?" was the question voiced by at least four of us.

"Did you guys practice that, or was it natural?" She shook her head and continued on. "The tendrils. They come down and feel around everywhere they can." As if on cue, we heard Tobias yell from down the hall. Since I was closest to the door, I got up, looked out, and let out a loud "ha!"

"It's the tendrils. They're poking around and Tobias looks as unhappy as can be to have them around. Oop, here they come." We all stood and moved aside as the tendrils felt around. We had already learned in a short time, if we left the tendrils alone, they generally left us alone. After a few minutes of being poked, prodded, and having two chairs toppled over, the tendrils finally left.

"We need to do something about those things," Sk'lar announced.

"I agree," Rouhr said. "And I believe that's the point Tella was trying to make. We're trapped, and we're being searched. We don't know what for, but we need to either figure it out or find a way to prepare for a long hold-out. So, we need plans. Every single plan you can come up with, no matter how stupid, asinine, or insane…it may turn out to be brilliant." He let out a deep breath. "That will be all."

We left the conference room and I gave Tella a light kiss on the cheek as she headed back to the lab. Takar and I left the building.

"Any thoughts on our assignment, brother?" he asked.

"Yep, and they're all stupid," I laughed. He joined me in my laughter. "You hungry?" I asked.

"Always."

"Good. I'm starving," I chuckled. "One favor, though?" I asked politely as we headed towards our favorite little shop.

"What's that, brother?"

"Don't make me eat a salad, I've had enough green the past few days." I did my best to keep a look of innocence on my face, but when he stopped walking to glare at me, I burst out laughing.

"You're an idiot," he snapped with a smile.

I kept laughing. That was possible.

But if so, I was a happy one.

EPILOGUE: TELLA

A week had passed since the vines overtook Nyheim. At first, I'd spent night and day inside General Rouhr's lab testing and retesting samples, looking at the same data for hours on end for something I might've missed the first time.

The first time I went to collect samples from the vines, I was nervous. Never in my wildest imaginings did I think one of the planet's native plants could grow to this size.

I read the initial reports done by Karzin and Annie when they first discovered the Puppet Master in the crater. The crater in which it resided was half a mile wide, suggesting that the creature we were dealing with was huge.

But this...

I looked out the window of the lab, where a towering wall of green rose up behind the buildings. I craned my neck in an attempt to see the top, but I couldn't. I made my way back to my desk, passing Leena, who was working around the clock as well.

"I'm running out of tests to run. I don't even know what I'm looking for at this point," she sighed.

"No luck with recreating the toxin?" I asked.

"I have pieces of it," Leena sighed. "The samples I tested were too small and the substance wasn't fully recognized by any of my machines. I should've gone to the *Aurora* to test the samples in the first place."

I pondered a moment in silence, both of us trying to come up with answers, possible guesses. Anything.

"Without another sample of that toxin, we're basically taking shots in the dark," Leena went on.

"At least we can satisfy some scientific curiosity," I suggested.

"Even that has its limits. I've just about figured out everything I'm going to figure out about the Puppet Master for now," Leena replied.

"I still have a few tests I can run," I replied. "They won't help our current situation, but maybe the knowledge will come in handy later."

"One can only hope," Leena muttered. I left her to

grumble over her data. I suddenly felt the urge to take a walk. I hadn't been in the lab very long, but I was already itching for some fresh air. I left General Rouhr's building without telling anyone where I was going, not that there was anywhere to go.

I walked through the city, my eyes trained up at the green vine dome that blocked out the sky. General Rouhr had had special lights built to make up for the lack of sunlight. They were huge, glowing white orbs that hung high above the buildings, almost touching the vines. It wasn't as nice as real sunlight, and everything had a green tinge to it now, but it was better than darkness.

I didn't stop walking until I reached the base of the vines. I'd been this close to the bases once before, the day the vines grew. That was to examine them and sample them with a scientific eye. I didn't take the chance to stand still and just look at them.

The vines were thicker than a building in some places, but as they stretched up, they wove together in intricate latticework that was a clear indicator of conscious design. It was too neat, too organized, and too beautiful to be the product of random growth.

Not long ago, being trapped against my will inside the boundaries of a city for an unspecified amount of time would've been my worst nightmare.

Then I met Rokul.

Ironically, he hated feeling idle and stuck just as much as I did, yet it was he who taught me that standing still for a little while is okay.

He hadn't asked about my family since I told him they were dead. Truthfully, I wasn't ready to talk about them yet. But I was ready to think about them, to remember them. I kept myself moving from place to place non-stop because I was too scared to think about them. The moment I stood still, images of the last time I'd seen them flooded me. That used to terrify me. Now, it wasn't scary, just painful.

I pressed my hand against one of the vines. It was solid, impenetrable, but softer than I'd expected it to be. I could feel the creature connected to these vines humming with life through my fingertips. Maybe that should've frightened me, but instead, it made me feel less isolated.

I stood completely still and closed my eyes, focusing only on the feel of the vines beneath my fingers. I let images of my family flood my mind's eye. I saw my little sister begging to come along when I went to explore the chunk of forest behind our house. She didn't like dirt, insects, or anything to do with nature, but she still always wanted to come.

My mom and my dad used to watch us from their kitchen window because they knew more about the dangers of the forest than we did. They still let us explore, because the last thing they wanted to do was teach us to be afraid of the world we lived in.

My throat constricted as a shuddering sob escaped my lips. At first, I tried to hold everything in. Then I realized there was no point. I let myself cry at the base of the vines.

"Tella." Rokul grabbed my shoulders and pulled me against his chest. I wrapped my arms around his waist and hugged myself closer to him.

"What are you doing here?" My tears dried up. Crying in front of others, even Rokul, wasn't something I was ready for yet, either.

"I saw you leave the building. I figured I'd walk with you." He smiled down at me. "I always forget how fast a walker you are. You can dip between people like water. I lost you twice before I finally found you here."

"If I'd known you wanted to come with me, I would've waited." I managed a smile.

"You looked like you wanted a few moments to yourself," Rokul said. "I'm sorry if I disrupted you."

"You could never." I pressed the side of my head into his chest to listen to his heartbeat. All traces of my little outburst vanished. "I just came out here to look at the vines. I feel like we've been doing everything to them except looking."

"Any progress in the lab?" he asked.

"No," I frowned. "That toxin is our only lead and we don't have enough to fully reconstruct it synthetically."

"A partial reconstruction is better than no reconstruction," Rokul reasoned.

"You're right," I agreed. "I'm sure Leena's already on it."

Rokul released his embrace and offered his hand to me. I took it, enjoying the comfortable, familiar feeling of his hand.

Together, we walked along the boundary created by the vines. I walked directly next to the wall of green and stretched my free hand out to run my fingers along the velvet-like skin of the vines.

"You seem to be enjoying those," Rokul observed.

"I wish they weren't here," I replied. "However, I'm also glad they grew around the city and not through it. This plant is sentient. It could've killed everyone in Nyheim if it wanted to."

"You make it sound like the Puppet Master is more than sentient. You're making it sound intelligent," Rokul said.

"We've named it the Puppet Master for a reason," I shrugged. "It has dominion over the other sentient plants. That implies a higher level of intelligence."

"Well, if that's true," Rokul leaned past me and shouted, "thanks for not killing us all!" I tipped my head back and laughed.

"I don't think it can hear you," I chuckled.

"You don't know that," Rokul replied.

"You're right, I don't," I admitted. "All I know is that if I'm going to be trapped in Nyheim, I'm glad I'm trapped with you."

"Me, too," he smiled. "But I know you. In another couple of days, you'll be restless and threatening to claw your way through the vines with your bare hands."

"That does sound like me," I said after considering his words.

"The moment those vines are cleared, you're going to take off like a blaster shot," Rokul chuckled.

"I'll be dragging you behind me, so you better get ready to keep up," I replied.

"Good. Where will you be dragging me?" he asked. I chewed my bottom lip as I pondered the question.

"I think I'd like to head to the swamplands," I decided. "There are species of plants unique to that area that I haven't gotten the chance to study."

"I've spent some time out there," Rokul said. "It didn't seem that different from the rest of the forest, but then again, I was there to stop Xathi hybrids, not look at flowers."

"Good point," I nodded. "If we do make it out to the swamplands, promise me one thing."

"Anything." Rokul's eyes were bright and his smile was warm.

"If we happen to come across a Helmria Ithalma, please don't kill it."

LETTER FROM ELIN

Oh my goodness, Rokul and Tella are a blast to write. Something about characters that don't have filters on their mouths, even if they keep their hearts more guarded.

It's possible I've woken the cats a few times, giggling at those two.

You know the crew is going to be doing everything they can to get out, searching in every direction for a weakness.

But what they discover will reveal a part of Ankou that they never suspected existed...

Keep reading for a sneak peek!

XOXO,

Elin

SYLOR: SNEAK PEEK

Nesta
It has never been a good idea to scream in the tunnels.

The darkness had its secret inhabitants and sometimes shadows were more than what they seemed. The mere sound of footsteps was enough to draw unwanted attention in the cramped tunnels below Nyheim, and caution was the number one tool to carry if you wanted to survive in the underground. And if you ventured deep into the tunnels, you needed more than just caution.

You needed silence.

"SON OF A BITCH!" I cried out as loud as I could, looking down as blood trickled out my cracked fingernail.

Yes, just a fingernail.

But it was the last straw.

My voice echoed through the maze of tunnels behind me, but I didn't care if someone (or something) could hear me. My broken nail demanded all my attention, and I would scream as loudly as possible if that helped ease the pain.

Caution and silence?

Screw that.

Sitting down on a pile of rubble, flashlight strapped to my shoulder, I brought my finger up to my mouth and sucked on the blood as I grimaced. The coppery taste of my own blood made my stomach growl in protest, and I remembered once more just how hungry I really was.

For a moment, I wondered if any Xathi had survived the war. Maybe some of them had snuck underground, feeding on helpless prey while growing fat. I wouldn't mind having one of the bastards find me right now. I'd carve them up really good, light a fire, and make a career as a Xathi chef. I was pretty sure the spidery assholes would taste like crap, but as long as they weren't poisonous, I wouldn't complain. Light a fire, sprinkle some herbs on there, maybe some pepper, as well...

"Focus," I said to myself out loud, my voice bouncing

off the cramped walls of the tunnel. Imagination would do nothing to keep my belly full. Sighing audibly, I ran one hand through my hair, pushing it all back, and eyed the pile of rubble in front of me. Stones with jagged edges were blocking the entrance to a smaller tunnel, one I knew as well as the lines on the palm of my hand. That little burrow had been carved by me, after all, and it had been the place I had started calling home after the first Xathi incursions.

It wasn't the best place to live if you hated tight places. In fact, I didn't want to be here now.

But I needed food. And so I'd returned to find my old abode.

It wasn't cozy—it was nothing but a hole in the stone, one sheltered from view from the blankets I had hung by the entrance—but that was the place where I had stashed my dingy possessions. Not that I cared about possessions, truth be told. The only thing I cared about in that moment was the pack of dried meat I was certain was among my things.

And so, I got to work.

Down on my knees, I started pushing the rubble out of the way with both hands. Beads of sweat started appearing on my forehead, and my stomach growled louder and louder with each movement. After half an hour or so, though, the rubble finally gave way, creating a small entrance that allowed me to squeeze myself into my little burrow.

"You've gotta be shitting me," I said, ignoring the small pile of dirty clothing on the corner and focusing on the packet of dried meat. It sat abandoned in one of the burrow's corners, the package torn open by the edge of a stone that had fallen from the ceiling. Inside it, fat and happy insects were busy banqueting on whatever was left of the meat.

Gritting my teeth, I kicked the packet as hard as I could, hissing in frustration. I couldn't believe I had wasted so much time digging through the rubble just to find out worms had stolen my lunch. But what was a woman to do? In a world where spaceships brimming with spidery assholes fell from the sky, and even the plants themselves were doing their best to get rid of you, there was no other option but to be tough.

Squeezing myself out of the burrow, I collected my backpack from the floor and slung it over my shoulder. No use in crying over spilt milk...or lunch-eating worms, for that matter. Besides, I had survived worse. No parents, raised by a criminal, and then establishing myself as a high-ranking member of an underground gang: a true survivor's curriculum.

Life had never been easy, but if I were to be honest, I'd had it good for a while.

Being a skilled contrabandist had its perks, and the

underground was the perfect place for someone like me to thrive. Then, of course, came the Xathi...and after that, those stupid giant vines. Lifechanging events for the entire population, and even more so for those who dwelled underground.

The Xathi attacks had made sure food shortages started being a daily occurrence, and when the vine dome took over the city, it all got worse. My little burrow got destroyed by the vines moving underground and even Odeon, my mentor and leader of our gang, vanished. Sabre, our gang of rogues and misfits, pretty much disbanded without Odeon's leadership.

And without a leader and food, Sabre was nothing more than a pretty name.

But maybe getting the gang back together was exactly what I needed to do. Our members were competent, and I was pretty sure that, with some strategizing and team effort, we could rebuild whatever was left of the underground.

It was with that thought in mind that I made my way through the tunnels, this time being more careful about it. The underground was a pretty safe place, all things considered, as long you remained in the main caverns complex and the adjacent tunnels. If you ventured deeper, though, nobody could really guarantee your safety. As for me, I didn't mind trading safety for a little privacy.

"Nesta, where have you been?" An old man croaked, standing up as I reached the end of the tunnel. I could only see his silhouette, his figure outlined by the warm lights flooding the cavern behind me. "Have you been looking for food? I don't have anything to trade, but I—"

"No food, Samuel," I said as I walked past him, ignoring his outstretched hand. "Not today." I heard him curse something, but I paid it no heed. My mind was already at work as I tried to think of a way to bring the gang together.

The first step?

A visit to Buke's, a large tent at the end of the cavern that doubled as a bar and canteen. Of course, now that there was no food to go around, the place was nothing but a gathering place for the underground's hard-hitting drinkers. Whoever of the old crew had remained underground, they had to be there.

I made my way through a sea of tents and merchants' carts, ignoring everyone's pleas for food. They all knew me as Nesta, the right hand of the Sabre's leader, and they were probably thinking I had a stash of food hidden someplace deep in the tunnels. Yeah, as if.

"Alright, Nesta," I muttered under my breath, standing before Buke's entrance. "Time to show these assholes what you're made of." With a deep breath, I ducked under the entrance, nothing but a large canvas supported by two tall logs, and silence immediately took over the room.

"Hey, assholes," I grinned, hands in my pockets as I stared at the four guys huddled at a low table in the corner. They were sitting on dusty old pillows, their legs folded, and tall pitchers of diluted beer sat in front of them. Life wasn't going well for them, that much I could tell. Any other time, and I would've found them here laughing raucously, their cheeks already tinged a drunkard's red. As it was, their faces had been hollowed out by hunger, and their expressions were grim. "You look like shit, the lot of you."

"You're one to talk," Stupid Joe threw back at me, slowly getting up to his feet. A tall bald-headed man, he looked imposing right up to the point where you found even a kid could trick him. He was probably the most gullible person I had ever met, but he compensated by having the quickest fingers in the whole of the underground. He could snatch a purse from someone's pocket and nobody would notice. "Where the hell have you been, Nesta?"

"Me?" I said with a smirk. "I found a goldmine, and set myself up as the Queen of the Underground. I came here to invite you to my palace."

"Really?" Stupid Joe's eyes lit up. "Will there be food in your palace?"

"C'mon, man," one of the other men, Topan, sighed. "She's just messing with you."

"Oh," he said, lowering his head as he sunk back onto his pillow. He grabbed his beer with a sad expression, and his belly rumbled with a desperate tone.

"What do you want, Nesta?" Topan continued, this time turning his attention to me. He was slightly shorter than the other men, but he had the kind of attitude that made others follow him. "Did you come to share the food you have hidden? Because if not, you can turn around and crawl back to whatever hole you just came from."

"Is that your way of saying you miss me?" I said, deadpan. "You're not as stupid as those assholes out there, are you? You know damn well that I don't have any food hidden. If I had, you guys would have been the first to know."

"Would we?" he queried. "Because I remember Odeon and you keeping secrets from the rest of us all the time. Who's to say the two of you didn't stockpile food behind our backs?"

"Odeon's dead, asshole," I sighed.

"I know that," he shrugged. "Is that why you're here? Do you want to be the Sabre's newest leader?"

"I don't—"

"You were Odeon's little pet, sure, but that doesn't mean shit anymore. Sabre has disbanded." Locking his eyes on mine, he gritted his teeth. "And, for the record, Odeon was an asshole."

"He did what he needed to do," I tried, even though I already knew my words were useless. These guys' minds were already made up. "The underground thrived under him."

"Really?" Topan said. "The way I see it, he just used Sabre to lead a comfortable life. Now, don't get me wrong...I want a comfortable life as much as the next guy. I just don't think the way Odeon did it was the right one. We should have been making money off the assholes on the surface," he continued, pointing with his thumb toward the ceiling, "not surviving on the back of those on the underground."

"You're wrong about Odeon," I hissed.

"Am I?"

"Yeah, you are, you dipshit." Shaking my head, I closed my eyes for a second to gather my thoughts and then turned on my heels. "Fine, if you want to stay hidden in here, go right ahead. Good luck trying to survive on that piss you call beer."

Without giving them the time for a reply, I marched out of Buke's. For a moment, I simply stood there, taking in the sad scene in front of me. While before the

Xathi the underground thrived, now it looked more and more like a refugee camp with each passing day. I had no idea how the few hundred people that lived in here would survive, but I wasn't about to curl up on the floor and wait for my turn to die.

I was a survivor...and so I would survive.

Even if I had to do it on the surface.

Sylor

It had been nine days, and slightly more than eleven hours, since the city was entombed by the vines of the 'Puppet Master.' It had been eight days, and just under four hours, since General Rouhr tasked Strike Team Two with discovering a way through the vines and back into the 'outside' world.

We had made numerous attempts, seventeen to be exact, and thus far, nothing had worked. The frustration upon all of our minds was palpable and a nuisance. The very idea that a mere vegetable had been able to thwart our every attempt, our patently superior technology, was confounding and absurd.

Nothing that we had tried had amounted to anything more than a measly scratch, a scratch that was healed in less than an hour. Whatever this creature was, it was not something that followed the laws and sense of reality. It was my job, by the order of General Rouhr, to do what was necessary in order to find a way through the vines, and I was not about to let seventeen failures deter me.

The typical Valorni warrior was slap-dash and crude. He used his fists if he didn't have a blaster. He used a blaster and blasted his enemy with wild abandon and bloodlust.

That was not me.

I hated the stereotypical Valorni behavior.

I tried to be as precise as possible. It wasn't always easy. My speech differed from Axtin, but contact with humans kept me in practice of using some vernacular.

It had become apparent that standard weapons and attacks would not be enough. Even attacks that by all sense and reason should have worked, had failed. So, it was now time to begin the progression from conventional to the unconventional.

It was time for me to speak with the botanist and the chemist. I needed to work with Tella and Leena.

After I arrived at their joint laboratory on the other side of General Rouhr's building, I implored them to use their abilities and knowledge for any sort of assistance they could give. As I walked into the office they shared, I smiled as genuinely as I could. "Good afternoon, ladies."

Leena looked up from a small microscope and returned my smile. Hers was genuine and real, even though it had not been in her nature to be kind and affable. "Afternoon, Sylor. Was there anything you needed?"

"They always need something," Tella snapped from her corner. "They don't come to see us otherwise." I knew that she was attempting to make a joke, to be funny, but there seemed to be a bit of an underlying resentment to her words. Perhaps it was that Tella was not the sort to enjoy confinement, and the vines of this creature were doing exactly that.

"Tella," Leena admonished. Apparently, her statement truly had been an attempt at humor. Leena turned back to me and motioned me to come in. As I did, she left her station and approached me. "So, what can we do for you, Sylor?"

There was a small sense of gratification to hear her say my name. Many of the humans still only knew me as one of 'those aliens.'

I did not blame them for their reactions to me, I was one of the foreigners that had brought war and destruction to their home.

But still, acknowledgement of my person was appreciated.

"Dr. Dewitt," I responded. "I have been tasked with finding a way, conventional or not, through the vines. We have made seventeen separate attempts and have failed seventeen times. I come to you seeking advice and a new set of minds to think of ideas."

"Well, now aren't you all proper and civilized," Tella commented, a half-smile twisting her lips. She waved a hand. "I don't mean anything by it, I'm just not used to it. Takar tries to be all high-and-mighty when he talks to me, but he's almost as crazy as his brother. It's a bit odd, hearing it from a Valorni."

"Tella!" Leena said with a sharp look. "That's rude!"

I held up my hand to put an end to Leena's reprimand. "It's alright. She is entitled to her opinion." I looked over at Tella. "To answer your question, my mannerisms are my own. There is nothing more to it, nor do I intend any, as you put it 'high-and-mightiness'. Now, is that enough of an answer for you?"

Tella shrugged, nodded, then returned to what she had been working on when I entered. I turned my attention back to Leena. "Would you be able to assist me?"

Leena stood still for a few breaths before finally answering. "I don't know." She reached out and placed her hand on my arm as I started to turn away. "I didn't say that we won't. What I meant was that I'm not sure if we'll be able to help. If everything that you've done has failed, I'm not sure what we can do."

"With your expertise in chemicals," I nodded at Leena, "and your expertise in plant life," I added with a nod to Tella, "I hope to gain some additional suggestions as to what we may be able to do."

Tella gave a sort of half shrug and arched an eyebrow as she sat in her chair. "The only thing that I can think of that had any sort of effect was the toxin." She looked at Leena, a look of disappointment adorning her face. "But we don't have enough to use."

My hopes had been dashed before they had been given a glimmer of life. Leena sighed and walked to a small row of cabinets on a near wall. She unlocked a glass door and retrieved a small vial. "This is all that we have. It's not enough for what you need, and not enough for us to synthesize."

"Besides," Tella cut in, "I'm not sure we want to find more anyway."

"Why is that?" I asked.

She rose from her chair and looked out the only window in the lab. "Take a look out there," she instructed me. I stepped over to the window. Her finger pointed to the vines. "Those things came up, out of the ground, and barely caused any damage. I know that a few buildings were destroyed, and a few people died, but Puppet Master went out of its way to make sure that we were closed in, not hurt. What if that changes with the toxin?"

"And what if it does?" I asked.

She rolled her eyes and huffed. "I really wish you overgrown brutes would learn to think things through." She pointed to one of the massive pillar-like vines a few blocks over. "Think about what damage that one vine there could cause if it fell. Are you willing to risk that?"

"So, you're afraid of some collateral damage? Is that what you're saying?" I asked.

"Of course, that's what I'm saying," she practically shrieked. "What if some of that 'collateral damage' is a life? What if some of that damage is the death of a child, or one of your own? What then?"

Before I had the opportunity to answer, Leena added her own opinion and fear to the argument. "Tella's right. If the toxin works on the vines the way it worked on some of the other plants, the damage potential would be catastrophic."

"I understand that, but if it wasn't," I countered. "What if we used the toxin upon a small section of the vines, caused it pain, and the vines retreated? We must not allow ourselves to be locked away in a dome like prisoners with no attempt to fight back. This creature must be shown that we will not go lightly."

"You're an idiot," Tella huffed. "I want out."

"I apologize," I said. "I don't understand what you mean."

"What I mean," Tella said, punctuating each word with a tilt of the head, "is that I'm done with this. I will not participate in this. The potential harm to the city and her people is too big, too much. I won't be part of it." With that, she turned away from us and left, Leena trying to call her back.

Leena turned back to me. "She has a point. The damage that could result is…"

"I understand," I interrupted. "However, to surrender to an enemy, that is something that cannot be permitted. We cannot simply give in to this…this… creature and expect it to simply leave us alone. It is routinely invading everyone's homes with its tendrils. It has forced us to use auxiliary power sources, and we will soon be out of resources. What are we supposed to do then?"

"I don't know," Leena admitted.

"I ask for your help because you are one of the smartest people I have ever had the privilege of meeting, and we need to find a method of escape." I looked at Leena in earnest. "General Rouhr has tasked me with finding a way through the vines, and I require your intellect to find a way. What do you say? Can we make a more powerful version of the chemical grenade you created?"

She was hesitant, and I could see that she was unwilling to assist, but her sense of duty and understanding won through. She eventually nodded.

We began our work, and after many hours of toil, we finally had a chemical bomb that was, if our calculations were correct, the most powerful that either of us had ever come across.

"Thank you. I mean it," I said quietly as I gently, ever so gently, laid it into a case that we had created for its transport.

Leena merely nodded, the look on her face telling me everything I needed to know about her feelings. I placed a hand on her shoulder, thanked her for her assistance, and left, carrying the case with the bomb with me. I walked slowly and carefully towards our testing ground, hoping that this would be enough to accomplish the task at hand.

Nesta

I hated the surface.

It was noisy everywhere I went, so much I could barely hear my own thoughts. The whole city seemed to be submerged in a chorus of loud voices, and the growl of shuttle engines as they zoomed back and forth overhead didn't seem to help. Never mind the giant green dome of vines that encased the whole place. Just looking up at its domed surface made me feel as if I were a tiny fish in some creepy alien aquarium.

I kept the hood of my ragged cloak up, doing my best to blend in with the crowd, but I quickly realized I didn't need any of that. The crowded streets and back alleys were brimming with people, and everyone seemed too preoccupied about their daily lives to give a damn about some bony woman wearing a dirty old cloak.

"Sol Avenue," I read from a sign, doing my best to recall the city layout. If I followed the avenue, I should be able to find the farmer's market...which meant I should be able to find some food.

I was pretty sure that the vines had cut off the city from the rest of the planet, and that the city must've been running low on food, but I tried to keep my hopes up. As bad as the situation probably was, I didn't see anyone assaulting whoever committed the sin of carrying a bag of vegetables down the street. I took that as a good omen, silencing my inner critic as it tried to convince me that the surface idiots were just too civilized to do something as lowly as steal food.

At the end of the avenue, my heart started jumping happily as I saw dozens of street stalls lining the walls of buildings. Merchants called after the potential customers with loud voices, but few people stopped. Some of them glanced warily at the food carts that seemed to pop up every hundred feet or so, but almost everyone kept their heads low and carried on. Either people weren't going hungry, or they had no money to spend on food.

Well, I was definitely hungry, and the fact that I had no money was just a detail.

"Greetings, good sir," I said with the largest smile I could conjure, approaching one of the vendors. I had no idea how polite I should act when dealing with surface street vendors, but I quickly decided that being as pompous as I could was a great idea.

"Hey," he said, an annoyed expression on his face. He eyed me curiously and, pursing his lips, folded his arms over his chest. Then, with a quick gesture, he threw some old blanket over the fruit in his stall. "No money, no food."

"What? Who the hell said I didn't have any money?" I found myself saying, already clenching my fists.

"Have you looked in a mirror recently?" he continued, his serious expression giving way to a mocking grin. I noticed he was missing teeth as his lips curled up and, for a moment, I imagined how it'd feel to make him lose another tooth or two. "Where the hell have you crawled out from? A mine?"

"Who the hell—"

"Do I think I am?" he finished for me. "The guy who won't sell you any food...unless you can pay for it, that is."

"Of course I can pay," I lied. Credits really dropped in value after everything went to shit, at least when it came to the underworld, and I hadn't bothered with carrying any these past few weeks. Not a problem: I'd pay this asshole with my fists. "Show me the goods."

"The goods?" he snorted. "What are you? Some hardened criminal?"

Briefly, I wondered if his teeth would have any value in the underground market. Maybe I wasn't meant to be a Xathi chef, after all. Perhaps it was my destiny to become a vendor of handmade collars made out of assholes' teeth. Not my first choice but, hey, you don't get to choose the talents you're born with.

Shaking his head, the man finally reached for the blanket covering his fruit and pulled it back. I looked down, my fingers already twitching as I imagined myself with a big fat apple in my hands, but what I found wasn't what I was expecting.

"What the hell's that?" I asked, frowning as I realized he wasn't selling fruit, after all. There were round pieces of bread on a tray, but they seemed almost as old as I was, blots of a sickly green mold covering their cracked surfaces.

"Food," he responded, quickly throwing his blanket over the tray again. "Now, pay up or get out of my way."

"I'll spend my money somewhere else, asshole," I finally said, holding my chin up before turning my back to him. My stomach grumbled in protest, the moldy bread looking more appetizing with each passing second, but I held strong. If I was going to steal something, I definitely wouldn't settle for something that seemed more mold than bread.

Stalking away from the mold vendor, I ambled down the avenue while paying close attention to whatever the vendors were trying to sell. Almost all fruit looked as if it were slowly rotting, all bread seemed to have mold in it, and there was barely any meat to be seen. It seemed that life wasn't being kind for anyone.

"Excuse me, miss," I heard a tired voice say from right behind me, and I quickly turned around to find an old woman standing there. She was pushing a cart loaded with apples down the avenue, and even though the apples didn't look freshly picked, they sure as hell seemed edible. In fact, the more I looked at them, the more they started looking like the best damn thing on the entire planet.

Taking one step back, I jumped out of the woman's way and she slowly went back to pushing her cart, groaning with the effort. She looked frail and tired, her face covered with wrinkles. Someone's grandmother, of that I had no doubt. "Let me help you with that," I said, standing next to her and laying both my hands on the cart. "Where to?"

"Oh, bless you," she smiled, pointing with her finger straight ahead. "Just at the end of the street. I'm taking these to my son's stall. I would do it myself, but my bones...getting old, you see."

"I see," I said as I smiled back at her, happily letting her lead the way.

I couldn't help but notice how some people greedily stared at the apples in the cart, but none of them seemed as if they were about to try something. You'd think that a war against spider-psychopaths from outer space would have given the surface folk an edge, but they seemed pretty civilized. I wondered if that had something to do with the aliens that had settled in the city. The bastards looked tough enough, so if they had taken it upon themselves to maintain the order...

"Here we are," the old woman said, pointing to a stall right beside her. In it, a portly man in his fifties was busy haggling with a woman carrying two small kids. "I know it's not much, but..." Still smiling, the woman reached for her cart and grabbed one of the apples. She threw it in my direction and I caught it midair, my stomach immediately coming alive as I felt the smooth surface of the apple under my fingertips.

"Thank you!" I exclaimed, already burying my teeth into it, juice dripping down my chin. It tasted amazing, perhaps the best meal of my entire life. Apparently, going for days without food was a good method of improving one's palate.

Hunger *really* is the best sauce.

Busy with wolfing down the apple, I only noticed the old woman had disappeared when I was about to thank her once more. She had joined whatever argument her son was having on the other corner of the stall, and she had left her apple cart unattended. I was about to call to her when another idea crawled into my mind.

Holding the half-apple I still had between my teeth, I closed in on the cart and went for the apples. Being as discrete as I could, I started stuffing them inside my ratty blouse, hoping that the way I had my cloak wrapped around my body would be enough to hide my spoils.

"Sorry," I quietly mouthed, throwing one last look at the old woman before I turned around. I started going down the avenue hurriedly.

Guilt ruined any excitement I should have felt at the score.

Food was scarce.

Fresh fruit was a hot commodity in the underground marketplace, and I knew I'd make some good trades with the dozen apples I was carrying inside my blouse.

Worse-case scenario, I'd just eat them all.

Maybe the surface wasn't that bad, after all.

Maybe I should visit more often.

I made a sharp turn at the end of the street when I felt something tug on the back of my cloak. "What the...?" I muttered, a massive green hand grabbing me by the bicep. I was spun around fast, only to come face to face with a man way taller than I was. Except, of course, he wasn't a man.

At least, not a human.

There was intelligence in the way his eyes glinted, but his body looked far more powerful than anything I had seen before. Even though he was wearing what looked like tactical gear, I could almost *feel* the way his hard muscles rippled under the surface of his green skin. If he wanted, I had no doubt he could pick me up and break me over his knee like a twig.

I had to be careful around this one.

"You stole from that woman," the green alien said. "You're going to jail."

And, just like that, being careful was out of fashion.

Gritting my teeth, I laid one hand on his wrist and, applying some pressure on the articulation, peeled his fingers off my shoulder. Then I gained as much balance as I could and sent my right foot flying against one of his ankles. The impact was brutal.

On me.

"Shit," I groaned, falling to the ground as pain travelled up my leg from my toes. "What are you made of? Stone?"

"I saw you steal from that woman," he declared, completely ignoring my totally relevant question. "Return those apples right now."

"What apples?" I asked, putting on what I hoped to be a look of pure innocence. It didn't help that, in that moment, the apples I had tucked inside my blouse rolled out from under me, one of them stopping right before the green alien's feet.

Shaking his head, he sighed audibly. "You're coming with me," he said, grabbing me by the scruff of my neck to pull me to my feet. As he did it, I noticed that he wasn't alone. There was a blonde woman with him, and she was already busy with picking my apples from the ground.

Defeated, I watched as she went back to the old woman's stall to return them. When she came back, I presented her with my best frown. She just ignored me, strutting down the avenue with the boundless energy that came with a full stomach.

"What now?" I asked my green captor as he pushed me down street, trailing after the blonde woman.

"Now you shut up," was all he said.

It was official: the surface sucked.

GET SYLOR NOW!

HTTPS://ELINWYNBOOKS.COM/CONQUERED-WORLD-ALIEN-ROMANCE/

PLEASE DON'T FORGET TO LEAVE A REVIEW!

Readers rely on your opinions, and your review can help others decide on what books they read. Make sure your opinion is heard and leave a review where you purchased this book!

Don't miss a new release! You can sign up for release alerts at both Amazon and Bookbub:
bookbub.com/authors/elin-wyn
amazon.com/author/elinwyn

For a free short story, opportunities for advance review copies, release news and the occasional cat picture, please join the newsletter!
https://elinwynbooks.com/newsletter-signup/

And don't forget the Facebook group, where I post sneak peeks of chapters and covers!

https://www.facebook.com/groups/ElinWyn/

Given: Star Breed Book One

When a renegade thief and a genetically enhanced mercenary collide, space gets a whole lot hotter!

Thief Kara Shimsi has learned three lessons well - keep her head down, her fingers light, and her tithes to the syndicate paid on time.

But now a failed heist has earned her a death sentence - a one-way ticket to the toxic Waste outside the dome. Her only chance is a deal with the syndicate's most ruthless enforcer, a wolfish mountain of genetically-modified muscle named Davien.

The thought makes her body tingle with dread-or is it heat?

Mercenary Davien has one focus: do whatever is necessary to get the credits to get off this backwater mining colony and back into space. The last thing he wants is a smart-mouthed thief - even if she does have the clue he needs to hunt down whoever attacked the floating lab he and his created brothers called home.

Caring is a liability. Desire is a commodity. And love could get you killed.

https://elinwynbooks.com/star-breed/

ABOUT THE AUTHOR

I love old movies – *To Catch a Thief*, *Notorious*, *All About Eve* — and anything with Katherine Hepburn in it. Clever, elegant people doing clever, elegant things.

I'm a hopeless romantic.

And I love science fiction and the promise of space.

So it makes perfect sense to me to try to merge all of those loves into a new science fiction world, where dashing heroes and lovely ladies have adventures, get into trouble, and find their true love in the stars!

Copyright © 2018 by Elin Wyn

All rights reserved. These books or any portion thereof may not be reproduced or used in any manner whatsoever without the express written permission of the Author except for the use of brief quotations in a book review.

This book is a work of fiction. Any similarity between the characters and situations within its pages and places or persons, living or dead, is unintentional and co-incidental.

www.ingramcontent.com/pod-product-compliance
Lightning Source LLC
Chambersburg PA
CBHW070735180626
46818CB00007B/2860